hooked on
a feline

TITLES BY SOFIE KELLY

hooked on a feline

A MAGICAL CATS MYSTERY

SOFIE KELLY

BERKLEY PRIME CRIME
new york

BERKLEY PRIME CRIME
Published by Berkley
An imprint of Penguin Random House LLC
penguinrandomhouse.com

Copyright © 2021 by Penguin Random House LLC
Penguin Random House supports copyright. Copyright fuels creativity, encourages diverse
voices, promotes free speech, and creates a vibrant culture. Thank you for buying an
authorized edition of this book and for complying with copyright laws by not
reproducing, scanning, or distributing any part of it in any form without permission.
You are supporting writers and allowing Penguin Random House to continue to
publish books for every reader.

BERKLEY is a registered trademark and BERKLEY PRIME CRIME and
the B colophon are trademarks of Penguin Random House LLC.

Library of Congress Cataloging-in-Publication Data

Names: Kelly, Sofie, 1958- author.
Title: Hooked on a feline: a magical cats mystery / Sofie Kelly.
Description: First Edition. | New York: Berkley Prime Crime, 2021. |
Series: Magical cats; 13
Identifiers: LCCN 2021019376 (print) | LCCN 2021019377 (ebook) |
ISBN 9780593199985 (hardcover) | ISBN 9780593200001 (ebook)
Subjects: GSAFD: Mystery fiction.
Classification: LCC PR9199.4.K453 H66 2021 (print) |
LCC PR9199.4.K453 (ebook) | DDC 813/.6—dc23
LC record available at https://lccn.loc.gov/2021019376
LC ebook record available at https://lccn.loc.gov/2021019377

First Edition: September 2021

Printed in the United States of America
1 3 5 7 9 10 8 6 4 2

Book design by Kelly Lipovich

hooked on
a feline

chapter 1

The stage set up at the end of the marina parking lot was in darkness, and there wasn't enough light from the stars and the sliver of gleaming moon overhead to make out anything, even though we were sitting just a few rows back. The crowd spread out across the pavement on lawn chairs and coolers had gone silent, so silent it seemed as though we were all holding our breath. But underneath that silence I could feel a faint buzz of anticipation, like the current of energy in the air just before a thunderstorm hits.

And then a clap of wood on wood, one drumstick hitting another, counting off the beat—*One! Two! Three! Four!*—cracked the quiet. And all at once there was music: the sound of a raucous electric guitar; and the crowd went wild. Beside me my friend Roma was grinning, bouncing on her canvas lawn chair, her dark eyes shining. She leaned sideways, bumping me with her shoulder. "That's Harry, Kathleen," she said in my ear, "which has to mean—"

She didn't get to finish the sentence because the smooth voice of the announcer boomed through the sound system, drowning out everything else. "Please welcome—after a very long absence—Johnny Rock . . ." He paused. I leaned forward, suddenly knowing what his next words had to be. And then they came: ". . . *and the Outlaws!*"

The stage lights came up and the crowd really went wild then, cheering, clapping, hooting and whistling. I couldn't take my eyes off the stage because that amazing electric guitar was in the hands of Harry Taylor—Harry, who mowed my lawn and kept just about everything running at the library for me. He was in his fifties with just a little hair left, his face lined from years of working outside in the sun. Harry looked like someone's dad, practical and dependable, which he was—not like some rock star guitar virtuoso—which it seemed he also was. I knew Harry played guitar. I knew he had been in a band, in *this* band, but I was dumbstruck that I had no idea he was so incredibly talented.

Roma was already moving to the music. "Close your mouth, Kath," she said, grinning as if she'd guessed what I'd been thinking. "I'm pretty sure you just swallowed a bug."

I didn't get a chance to answer because Johnny Rock had

started to sing John Mellencamp's "R.O.C.K. in the U.S.A.," striding onto the stage from the left side. His voice was full and strong with just a hint of a raspy edge to it.

Johnny Rock, aka John Stone, looked like he could have been actor Bradley Cooper's older brother—blue eyes, brown hair shot with a bit of gray waved back from his face, long legs and muscular arms in a tight black T-shirt and faded jeans. He had that same naughty-boy grin as the actor as well.

Harry was just behind Johnny's right shoulder, a few steps back. He, too, wore a black T-shirt and jeans, but not his ubiquitous Twins ball cap. I realized that he was playing the same solid-body Fender Stratocaster that he'd brought to Reading Buddies at the library, where he'd led the kids in an enthusiastic version of the Beatles' "Yellow Submarine." The song had been stuck in my head for days afterward.

Beside me Roma was already up and dancing. It seemed like the whole crowd was on its feet, spilling across the parking lot onto the grassy riverbank. Roma grabbed my hand and pulled me off my chair. "I can't believe they kept the whole band coming back together a secret."

"Me neither," I said, leaning sideways so she could hear me. Harry had been in the library just hours ago and there had been no hint from him that he'd be onstage tonight when I'd said I was looking forward to seeing Johnny in concert. I had no idea Harry was so good at keeping a secret. It seemed there were a lot of things I didn't know about Harry Taylor.

"Well, Mike checked my cracked tooth on Thursday and he

didn't give anything away, either," Roma said, raising her voice over the crowd noise.

Mike Bishop, who had expertly completed a root canal on my upper-left molar just recently, was also up onstage playing bass, standing behind and to the left of Johnny. Like Johnny and Harry, he was wearing jeans and a black shirt, along with a dark gray fedora over his gray curls. And he couldn't seem to stop grinning. He raised one arm in the air. "C'mon, people, you should be dancin'!" he shouted.

The outdoor concert was part of the Last Bash, a revival, after twenty-five years, of a summer festival celebrating food, music and small-town life. Mayville Heights was trying to bring back the celebration as a way to entice more tourists to our Minnesota town. The highlight of the event for just about everyone was the return to the stage of Johnny Rock, who had been a local celebrity in his teens and twenties, first as the lead singer of Johnny and the Outlaws and then as a solo performer. Johnny had gone on to become a very successful businessman. He had just sold his real estate development company and was going back to his first love, music.

I closed my eyes for a moment and just focused on Johnny's voice as the band segued into Boston's "More Than a Feeling." I draped my arm around Roma's shoulders and we swayed back and forth to the music, heads together like we were teenagers. The 1976 rock ballad showcased Johnny's vocal range. He was good—not just small-town-bar-band good—good enough to have had a career as a working musician, in my opinion. And I knew a little about the music business. My brother, Ethan, had his own band back in Boston, The Flaming Gerbils. I'd learned from watching his career develop how mercurial the music business could be, how it took more than talent, how sometimes it seemed that talent was the least important factor. I couldn't help wondering what had derailed Johnny's long-ago musical aspirations.

Roma was singing, "It's more than a feeling," softly by my ear. I opened my eyes. Next to Roma, her husband, Eddie, and our friend Maggie were dancing. I knew Mags could dance but I hadn't known that Eddie could. I shouldn't have been surprised. Eddie Sweeney was a former NHL player. He was tall and fast and smooth on his feet, even without skates.

To my right Marcus—my Marcus—was dancing with Mary Lowe. Mary was easily a foot shorter than he was and several decades older, but she had some smooth moves herself. She caught my eye, raised her eyebrows and gave me a saucy grin.

I smiled back at her.

"Best night ever," Roma said.

It was one of her favorite expressions, but she was right. This was going to be one of those nights I knew I'd remember for a long time.

The band came to their last song way too soon. "You know, I could stay out here all night," Johnny began.

"Do it!" a voice yelled from somewhere on the edge of the riverbank. There were echoes of the words all through the crowd.

Johnny smiled. "Believe me, I'd like to, but like they say, all good things must come to an end." He gazed out over the crowd. "Thank you all for coming tonight and I hope you liked my"—he turned and looked over his shoulder at the guys behind him—"our little surprise."

People started clapping again. I leaned back against Marcus's chest and he wrapped his arms around me. I wished the band *could* keep playing all night. I didn't want to be anywhere except where I was right now.

Johnny walked back to Mike and leaned an elbow on his friend's shoulder. Mike's hands were resting on his glossy black StingRay bass. He was about average height, with a stocky build and strong arms. He had a great mischievous grin, which he was giving to Johnny now.

"Mike and I met on the playground when we were what? Six years old?" Johnny asked.

"Seven," Mike said.

"Another kid, who I won't name"—Johnny coughed—"Thorsten." Everyone laughed. "Had just knocked out one of my front teeth with a swing. Mike looked all around and found the tooth in the grass. He gave it to me so the tooth fairy would come."

"Professional courtesy," Mike said, deadpan.

"We kinda lost touch for a while and then Mike came to audition for the band. And we've been friends ever since."

Mike looked up at Johnny. "You know, a good friend is like a good joc—" He stopped and held up one hand, a not-exactly-sincere expression of contrition on his face. "Sorry. This is a family venue. I'll start again. A good friend is like a good athletic supporter."

Johnny shook his head. "Really?" he said.

I wasn't sure if *he* knew the punch line to Mike's story but I knew there'd be one.

Mike nodded. "Absolutely. Not really very flashy." He raised an eyebrow. "No sequins. And sometimes makes you just a little uncomfortable." He held up a hand again. "But when life kicks you in the"—the drummer rolled a flourish on the cymbals—"you know you're always covered!"

Everyone laughed.

Mike pointed a finger at Johnny. "Love you, man."

"Friends to the end," Johnny said.

The two men fist-bumped and then Johnny moved toward the drummer. He ran a hand through his hair. "Paul and I met in detention," he began.

"We were set up," Paul called out.

More laughter.

Paul Whitewater was wiry with lean, strong arms in his black T-shirt and his bleached hair was cut very short.

"Now there are differing opinions on whether or not we deserved to be in detention," Johnny continued.

"That time," Mike added, deadpan.

Johnny narrowed his eyes at the bass player. "*That* time," he repeated. He turned his attention back to Paul. "My brief stint as a juvenile delinquent not withstanding, I couldn't have found a better drummer or a better friend."

"Back at you, brother," Paul said.

Ritchie Gonzalez was the band's keyboard player. He was stocky and solid with dark eyes, dark hair and olive skin. He wore a black leather cuff on his right wrist and a silver skull bracelet on his left. The bottom of a tattoo peeked out from the edge of his T-shirt sleeve. "Hey, Johnny," he said with a smile.

Johnny smiled back at him. "Ritchie and I met in church."

"And the building *wasn't* struck by lightning," Mike interjected.

Johnny shot him a look but it was clear from his body language and the hint of a smile pulling at his face and eyes that he wasn't really mad. "You're going to get struck by something if you're not careful," he said.

Mike folded his arms over his instrument again and dropped his head but he couldn't completely rein in his grin, so once again his contrite act didn't quite work.

Johnny gave his head a little shake. "As I was saying, Ritchie and I met in church. It was during the music festival and there were about three classes' worth of kids down in the basement of St. Bartholomew's waiting for our turn to perform. Ritchie was fiddling around on this old organ he'd found down there."

"It was a Yamaha A55 Electone," Ritchie said. "Someone had probably donated it to the church."

"I'm sure they had no idea what they were starting." Johnny gestured at Ritchie. "So I'm standing there, looking oh so cool in my white shirt and bow tie." There was a ripple of laughter.

"Thank you, Mom, for making me wear it to every music festival I was ever in. And Ritchie—who I'd like to point out was not wearing a bow tie—started playing 'Light My Fire.' And I started singing."

Ritchie frowned. "Did you tell them we were in a church?"

Even from several rows back, I could see the gleam in Johnny's dark eyes. "And it was very shortly after our time at St. Bartholomew's that we met Paul. But you know that part of the story." His words got yet another big laugh. Next to me Eddie gave a two-fingered wolf whistle. Roma leaned against his side, her head on his shoulder and her arm draped across his back.

There was only one band member left. "Harry Taylor," Johnny said. Harry smiled at him. Johnny looked out over the crowd. "Do you want to know how long I've known this guy?" he asked.

"Yes," I called out. So did a lot of other people.

"When I met him, he had hair," Johnny said. "Lots of it."

Harry smoothed a hand over his almost bald head.

"The first time I heard this guy play, it was on a guitar he got from the S&H Green Stamps catalogue. And even then it was magic." Johnny clapped a hand on Harry's shoulder and they exchanged a look. They had the kind of easy connection that comes with old friends. "We've been friends longer than I sometimes want to admit to and I don't know a better person."

Johnny held out a hand, gesturing at the band. "These guys are more than just my friends: They're my brothers." He raised his arm in the air and Mike began to run a bass line. Harry joined in on guitar followed by Ritchie and Paul and they moved into a song that I'd never heard before with Johnny covering every inch of the stage as he sang.

When you can't find the way,
And you can't see the road,
When your heart is too heavy
To carry the load,
When you can't find your voice,
When the darkness won't go,
When you're looking for somewhere to lay your weary head down
I'll be your home.

At the end of the song the other four members of the band joined Johnny at the edge of the stage to take a bow, arms around one another's shoulders. The crowd stayed on their feet, cheering and clapping, even after the men had all left the stage. I could see that they weren't going to let the band get away without another song.

The lights dimmed a little and Ritchie walked out from somewhere backstage. "Thank you," he said, waving at everyone as he slid behind his keyboard. He started to play a melody that I knew, but in the moment couldn't place.

Mike came out of the wings from the left side of the stage. He picked up his bass and put the strap over his head. "We love you!" he shouted to the crowd as he started to play.

Harry came out next, carrying his Martin twelve-string. He raised one hand in recognition of the applause, which seemed like it was never going to end, before picking up the melody from Ritchie. Paul was right behind Harry, blowing a kiss to everyone before sitting down at his drum kit.

Johnny was singing before he was onstage—"I'll Stand by You," written by the Pretenders' Chrissie Hynde.

I swayed in time to the music and sang along softly with Johnny, wrapped in the warmth of Marcus's arms.

This time when the guys left the stage, everyone seemed to understand that they wouldn't be back again. Still, people seemed reluctant to leave as if, somehow, the spell the band had cast over the evening would be broken.

"Tired?" Marcus asked.

I shook my head. "No. I have all this energy I don't know what to do with. I know I couldn't sleep."

Roma cocked her head to one side, tucking a strand of dark hair behind her ear. "I know Eric was planning on staying open late," she said. "How about dessert? Or really, really early breakfast?" She turned and looked over her shoulder at Maggie.

Maggie's green eyes narrowed. "Do you think there might be more of that fruit cobbler we had the other day at lunch?"

Roma smiled. "There's only one way to find out for sure."

Brady Chapman was standing next to Maggie. I saw her reach for his hand and raise a questioning eyebrow. The two of them were . . . I didn't really know what they were. Maggie insisted they weren't a couple but they spent all their free time together and neither of them was seeing anyone else. Mary Lowe liked to say they were "keeping company."

"It works for me," Brady said now.

Roma looked toward me again. I glanced up at Marcus, who nodded. "Let's go," I said.

Marcus grabbed our chairs. I looked around for Mary to say good night, but she'd already disappeared. We headed across the parking lot, all veering off in different directions because we'd all parked in different places. Roma and Eddie had gotten to the marina early to save a place for the rest of us and they'd managed to snag a spot close to the building. I'd parked my truck on a nearby side street. Based on the direction Brady and Maggie—who were already ahead of everyone else—were headed, they'd done the same thing.

When we got to Eric's Place, the café wasn't as busy as I'd expected. Nic, who generally worked nights, showed us to my favorite table in the front window. He was three or four inches taller than my five-six with a solid frame, deep brown eyes and light brown skin. "You just came from the Last Bash concert, didn't you?" he asked. Like Maggie, Nic was an artist. He created assemblages with metal and paper—things most of us recycled or threw away—and he was also a very talented photographer.

"It was incredible," Brady said.

"And it's true the whole band was there?"

Roma nodded. "You wouldn't believe how talented Harry Taylor is on guitar or Mike Bishop on bass."

Nic stared at her. "Dr. B. plays bass with the Outlaws? No way. You're kidding."

"Uh-uh," I said, taking one of the chairs closest to the window. "He's really good, too."

"He did my root canal last winter. Why didn't I know he'd played with Johnny Rock?"

Roma smiled. "Probably because the last time Johnny and the Outlaws played together you were a baby."

Nic grinned back at her. "Good point, but it doesn't mean I'm not a little jealous that I didn't get to see them tonight."

"So you'll get to see them next time," Maggie said, looking down at the dessert menu Nic had handed her when she sat down.

"Next time?" I turned to look at her. So did everyone else.

"Do you know something the rest of us don't?" Brady asked.

Maggie looked up at us. "What? No. No. It's just that everyone who was there tonight could see how much fun the guys were having. I can't believe they're just going to do that once and then walk away."

I thought about how often I'd noticed Harry smiling tonight and how Paul and Mike couldn't stop grinning. "You might be right," I said.

Nic was still smiling. "I hope you are." He gestured at the menu Maggie still held in one hand. "So what can I get for you?"

"Is there any more of that cobbler you had on Wednesday?" she asked.

"The strawberry rhubarb?"

Maggie nodded.

Nic's dark eyes sparkled. "Eric just took some out of the oven about twenty minutes ago. It's still warm."

"That would be perfect," Maggie said.

He looked around the table. "For everyone?"

We all nodded our agreement, looking a little like a collection of bobblehead dolls. "Please," I said.

Nic traced a circle in the air with one finger, working his way around the table. "Coffee, coffee, coffee, coffee, coffee and tea?" He ended the circuit at Maggie.

"I think I'll have tea, too," Roma said.

"I'll be right back," Nic said, heading for the kitchen.

Across the table from me, Roma was swaying from side to side, the motion so small, it was almost unnoticeable.

"Okay, so what song are you still hearing in your head?" I asked.

Her cheeks turned pink. "'Hold On,'" she said. "Hold On" was one of several songs the band had performed that had been written by Johnny and Mike. Johnny and the Outlaws had mostly been a cover band I knew, but they had performed some of their own songs as well. "I was remembering the first time I heard Johnny sing it. It was the very first time I saw them in concert. That was a long time ago."

Roma was older than the rest of us, although it wasn't something I ever thought about. I knew she'd seen Johnny and the

Outlaws in concert more than once before the band had broken up.

A smile pulled at her mouth and there was a faraway look in her eyes. "I was sixteen. They were playing at the high school in Red Wing—opening for some other group, and for the life of me, I can't remember who it was. What I do remember vividly is that Johnny had hair to his shoulders, Mike had a mullet and they were way better than the band they were opening for."

I tried to picture Mike Bishop with a mullet but couldn't get there. Then again, before tonight I would have never been able to picture him playing bass in a band, either.

"If they were that good, why did they break up?" Brady asked. Brady was a lawyer. He had a very practical, logical streak.

Roma frowned. "I don't know. I just always assumed that real life got in the way. I don't imagine any of their parents thought being in a band would be a good career choice."

"I saw them in concert right before they broke up," Maggie said. "I was maybe six."

"What were you doing at a concert when you were six?" Roma asked.

She shrugged. "My dad was a big music fan. I don't mean it was at a club or anything close to that. The show was in the daytime. I know we were outside somewhere and Dad bought me a caramel apple. I have no idea what songs they did but I do remember that caramel apple. It was good."

Marcus leaned back in his chair. "I saw Johnny on his own in a little club in Minneapolis. I was eighteen. I had a fake ID. It was just Johnny and another guy playing guitar."

Eddie gave him an incredulous look. "You had a fake ID? You? Mr. Law and Order?"

Marcus was a detective with the Mayville Heights Police Department. Pretty much everyone in town would have described him as a straight arrow. "It was during my bad-boy phase."

Roma burst out laughing. She held up one hand and pressed the other against her chest. "I'm sorry, Marcus," she said. "I just . . . I just can't picture you having a bad-boy phase."

"Hey, I had long hair and a couple of days of scruff, and I wore Docs with everything . . . and okay, so I probably wasn't nearly as rebellious as I thought I was."

"No, you weren't," Brady said emphatically. "Ever spend the night in jail?"

"Yes," Marcus said. That got everyone's attention. "It was during training."

Brady shook his head. "Yeah. Doesn't count. Ever been chased by the police?"

"Oh! I have." Eddie waved one hand in the air.

Maggie didn't say anything, but I noticed she nodded her head ever so slightly. Had she been chased by the police at some point in her past? It seemed about as likely as Marcus ever having been a "bad boy."

"Who are you people?" Roma asked. "And why didn't

I know my own husband seems to have had a run-in with the law?"

"I told you that story," Eddie said. "Back when I was playing. We were on the road in Chicago. Matts ended up naked. Remember?"

For a moment she still looked confused, then recognition dawned on her. "It was February. You were trying to snag the last playoff spot that year."

Eddie nodded, leaning back and resting both wrists on the top of his head. "Though technically that might not count as the only time I was chased by the police. It depends on how you define 'chased.'" He paused for a moment. "And 'police.'"

Eddie was saved from having to explain himself any further by Nic arriving at the table with our food. The strawberry-rhubarb cobbler was as delicious as it had been when Maggie, Roma and I had enjoyed it on Wednesday. It was still slightly warm from the oven, with a small dollop of vanilla-flavored whipped cream.

No one spoke until we'd all eaten pretty much half of our desserts. Then Maggie turned to Roma, holding up her spoon as though it were a magic wand that she was about to grant a wish with. "This was such a good idea," she said. "Thank you for suggesting we come here."

Roma smiled at her. "I can't believe Johnny got the band back together and no one figured it out."

Marcus shrugged. "Maybe there were people who did, but just didn't want to ruin the surprise."

I set down my spoon and reached for my coffee. "I can't get over how Harry didn't give himself away." I was pretty good at spotting subterfuge. My parents were actors and I'd learned a lot about the subtleties of body language from them. "I told him how much I was looking forward to hearing Johnny perform and all he said was so was he."

"Which wasn't a lie," Roma said, licking whipped cream from the back of her spoon. "He just didn't say he'd be performing as well."

"Good point," I said. "And it was an incredible surprise. I'm glad everyone who knew kept the secret."

"You should tell Harry that," Maggie said. She scooped up a piece of rhubarb and swirled it through the whipped cream in Brady's bowl. She'd already eaten all of hers. His response was to nudge the dish a little closer to her without saying a word.

I took a sip of my coffee. "I will, the very next time I see him."

Mags lifted the lid of her little teapot and peered inside, then closed it again, seemingly satisfied with what she'd seen. She looked at me and gestured over her shoulder. "Just look over at the door," she said with a smile. "Harry just walked in."

chapter 2

Harry, Johnny and the rest of the Outlaws had just come in. Nic walked over to them, looking around the room as he did so. He said something to Johnny, who nodded, and the group started in our direction. Ritchie had his arm around a tiny, dark-haired woman. His wife, I guessed. Paul was holding hands with *his* wife, Sonja, whom I knew from the library.

There were two smaller tables to our left. Nic pushed them together and quickly rearranged the chairs, grabbing a couple extra from a nearby table.

Mike was still wearing his fedora. He dropped it on the nearest chair. Roma was already on her feet. Mike grinned, raising one eyebrow at her. His face was flushed. She hugged him and then pulled back and slugged his left arm. "You are such a sneak," she said. "I can't believe you kept a secret like that."

"Was it worth it?" Johnny asked.

Roma nodded. "Absolutely!"

"Your playing gave me goose bumps," I said to Harry.

He smiled. "Thank you," he said. He shifted from one foot to the other almost as though he was a bit uncomfortable hearing the praise.

Nic had come back with the coffeepot and was filling cups at the table.

"Do you think we could get breakfast sandwiches?" Johnny asked him.

Nic nodded. "Sure. Sourdough and fried tomatoes?"

"Sounds good," Johnny said. "Thanks."

Nic glanced at me and then dropped his gaze down to my mug for a moment. I nodded. He made his way over and topped up my cup and Brady's. "It shouldn't be too long," he said to Johnny as he headed back toward the kitchen.

Johnny turned to me. "So?" he asked, holding up both hands. Johnny was what my mother would have called "one of the good ones." It wasn't common knowledge, but he was a big supporter of the elementary school's brown-bag lunch program and Reading Buddies at the library.

"So 'wow' doesn't seem anywhere near adequate," I said.

He smiled. "Thank you. There was something magical

about being up onstage with the guys again." He rolled his eyes. "I know it probably sounds silly, talking like that."

I shook my head. "Not to me. Both my parents are actors and I've seen firsthand that sometimes the whole really is more than the sum of its parts."

Mike joined us then. "Hi, Kathleen. How's your tooth?" he asked. He couldn't seem to keep still. The fingers on his right hand were moving like they were still on the strings of his bass. He reminded me of my brother, Ethan.

"My tooth is fine and you were terrific," I said.

"Thank you," he said, giving me that little-boy grin.

"How did you manage to keep the reunion a secret?"

Johnny shifted from one foot to the other. Like Mike he still seemed to have that buzz of energy from the concert. "I still can't believe that we did. Mostly it was just dumb luck. I figured someone would mess up and it would get out."

"He means me," Mike said. "Hey, Kathleen, you know those old World War Two posters you have down at the library?"

I nodded.

Roma's husband, Eddie, had opened a hockey school in Mayville Heights. A cache of Second World War propaganda posters had been unearthed during renovations to the empty warehouse down by the river that was home to the school. Eddie had donated them to the library. I had an exhibit of the posters planned for November, and after that, they were going to be auctioned off with the proceeds going to our ongoing project to digitize all the old documents we had that were too fragile to be handled very often. The posters were in excellent shape and I was hoping they'd all sell.

Mike stuck out his lower lip and plucked at it several times with one finger like he was playing a guitar string. "'Loose lips sink ships,'" he said, quoting one of the posters he'd seen in my office. Mike was working on researching his family tree and he'd spent a lot of time at the library recently, going though old records and documents. "Everyone thought I'd never be able to keep quiet. And you were all wrong."

"I'm impressed by your secret-keeping skills," I said.

Mike put one hand on his chest and gave a slight bow. "Thank you," he said.

"Yeah, you did good," Johnny said. He looked at me. There was a gleam in his blue eyes. I had the feeling Johnny just might have used Mike's desire to prove everyone wrong to make sure their secret stayed secret.

Nic came from the kitchen then with a giant circular tray. I could smell Eric's signature breakfast sandwich and I almost wished I had ordered one instead of the cobbler.

I sat down again and picked up my coffee. Eddie had shifted in his seat and was deep in conversation with Paul Whitewater, who had turned his own chair sideways, and Brady, who was standing by the end of our table, hands jammed in his pockets. They had to be talking about hockey, I realized, based on the way Eddie was moving his hands almost as though he were holding a stick.

After more than one setback, the Sweeney Center was finally finished. The former warehouse space had an ice surface and a conditioning room. Eddie would start working with his first class of summer hockey students on Monday. Roma had told me that he was also donating coaching time and space to both the boys' and girls' high school hockey teams. That didn't surprise me. That was the type of person Eddie was.

Sonja Whitewater was sitting beside her husband. She leaned sideways into my line of vision and waved. I waved back; then I stood up again and made my way over to her, carrying my coffee.

"So did you enjoy the concert?" Sonja asked. She had ice-blue eyes and blond hair cut to her collarbone.

"I don't know when I last had so much fun," I said.

She grinned. "I'm glad. I've always been more nervous than Paul is when he performs."

I nodded. "I know what you mean. My mom and dad are actors and Mom is always more anxious when Dad's performing than she is when she's the one onstage. And heaven help any critic who doesn't like his work."

Sonja laughed. "I think I'd like your mother. I'm exactly the same way. I'm glad you're here. I've been wanting to thank you for the book recommendations last time I was in. They were all a big hit, especially the series about the talking hamster named Einstein."

"It's one of my favorites," I said. "I'm glad you like it. And in case you're interested, we have multiple copies of all the books in the series so far."

"I can't tell you how glad I am to hear that," she said. "I would never complain about my kids reading but we go through books the way other families go through boxes of Cheerios."

"Kids who like to read," I said with a smile. "Music to my ears."

Sonja's phone buzzed then and she reached for it. "I'll see you Monday," she said.

Harry was seated on the other side of the two pushed-together tables from Sonja and Paul. Ritchie Gonzalez and his wife were on his left and there was an empty seat to his right. I made my way over to Harry. There was something I wanted to do.

"Harry, I owe you an apology," I said when I reached him.

He frowned. "Why? What did you do?" He indicated the chair beside him and I sat down.

"I kept you at the library, going on about my ideas for the cold frames this afternoon, and you had the concert to get to."

Harry was shaking his head before I finished speaking. "You don't have to apologize for anything. As I remember it, it was me who asked you to come out and show me where you want to put those boxes."

Harry had built several raised beds so the kids in our summer program at the library could grow their own vegetables. The project had turned out to be more successful than I'd hoped. We'd made salads with the first harvest of lettuce and

radishes and not one child had complained about eating vegetables. A couple of days ago, we'd sent each child home with a
small bag of tomatoes and yellow beans. I wanted to extend the
growing season with cold frames so the Reading Buddies kids
could have the same experience.

"Kathleen, you don't know Ritchie and Elena, do you?"
Harry asked.

I shook my head. "I don't."

He gestured at his friend. "Kathleen Paulson. Ritchie and
Elena Gonzalez."

I smiled. "It's nice to meet you both."

Elena had a mass of dark curls brushing her shoulders. She
was wearing a black T-shirt with the words *I'm with the band*
across the chest.

She looked familiar. I thought back to where I could possibly have met her before and then it hit me. "Are you a nurse?"

She smiled. "A nurse practitioner."

"You helped treat my broken wrist at the clinic about four
years ago. I knew you looked familiar," I said.

"That's right." She tipped her head toward my arm. "May
I?" she asked.

I nodded.

She reached over and gently fingered my left wrist. "It looks
like you healed well," she said.

"I did, although I now have a better accuracy rate predict-
ing rain than the meteorologist on Channel 4."

Ritchie smiled. "She never forgets a patient."

Elena shrugged. "I just have that kind of memory. I'm really good at trivia games, too."

"So am I," I said. "You know, we've been talking about doing a trivia tournament this winter at the library."

Ritchie looked at Harry. "You may have started something here."

Elena's dark eyes lit up. "We'll talk later," she said.

Ritchie leaned forward. "I think I saw you once in the library when I was meeting Mike. It's a gorgeous old building by the way."

"Thank you," I said. "It took a lot of work from a lot of people, including Harry."

Harry didn't say anything. He just gave his head a little shake. He was the most self-effacing person I had ever met.

"Kathleen, someone mentioned that Ethan Paulson is your brother," Ritchie said. Up close I could see some gray in his thick dark hair. "Is that right?"

"He is," I said. "How do you know Ethan?"

Ritchie smiled. Without a smile he looked more than a little imposing. With one he looked like a big teddy bear. "I don't really know him. I saw The Flaming Gerbils last winter in Red Wing and I got to talk to your brother between sets. Man, what a voice!"

I felt a rush of big-sister pride. I knew Ethan was enormously talented but it was always great to hear other people felt the same way.

"He would have loved tonight," I said. "You were all incredible."

"Thank you," Ritchie said. "It was a once-in-a-lifetime experience, getting out there again, all five of us together."

"Or maybe not."

I turned. Mike was standing behind me.

"Give it a rest," Ritchie said. He didn't seem annoyed by Mike's comment. I got the feeling he was mostly ignoring it.

Beside me Harry let out a breath. "Mike thinks we should all go out and do a few dates with Johnny," he said to me by way of explanation.

"You can't tell me you really don't want to do this again!" Mike exclaimed. "They loved us. You were there, Kathleen. Tell him!"

"Harry doesn't need me to tell him anything," I said, getting to my feet. "But I do need to tell you about a couple of resources I thought of that might be useful to help you finish your family tree." I tipped my head in the direction of the long counter at the other end of the diner and reached for my coffee. "I need a refill. Walk me over."

Mike rolled his eyes. "I know what you're doing," he said.

"I thought you would," I said. I smiled at Ritchie and Elena. "It was good to meet you."

"You too, Kathleen," Ritchie said. Elena nodded and smiled.

"So did you really come up with more ideas for me?" Mike asked as we made our way around the tables.

I nodded. "Actually the credit should go to Abigail. She remembered some documents that seem to be from some kind of accounting of people in this part of the state. We did a little digging and found them. They predate the first Minnesota Territorial Census of 1849 by a year. They might help you learn more about your great-great-grandfather's family."

"You're serious?"

I nodded. "The paper is very fragile and you'll need a magnifier and some patience to read the names."

"I thought I was at a dead end. This could be exactly what I've been looking for." Going on the road with Johnny seemed to be forgotten—at least for now. Mike gave me a saucy grin. "Kathleen, I would bow down and kiss your hand if your very large police-detective boyfriend weren't just over there talking to my cousin."

"How about you bring me coffee next time you come to the library instead?"

"Done!" he said. "And that will be Monday—probably afternoon if that's okay? I took the week off."

"It's fine with me. Abigail will be there and so will I."

Nic was behind the counter. He held out a hand and I gave him my mug. He refilled it and handed it back. "Thank you," I said.

Mike and I headed back to the others. "Hey, I really owe you a big thank-you for all the help you've given me while I've been researching the family," he said. "It turned out to be a much bigger project than I ever expected."

"It's part of my job," I said. "And I've found the whole thing fascinating." I took a sip of my coffee. "I had no idea your great-aunt, Leitha, went to college at sixteen, let alone learned to fly as part of the War Training Service. And she knew John Glenn."

"Yeah, that surprised me as well. She rarely talked about that part of her life." He pulled his fingers through his hair. "You know, Aunt Leitha is the reason I started researching the Finnamore family history."

I shook my head. "I didn't."

"Before she died she was taking part in a long-term study into heart disease."

"I *did* know that."

Leitha Finnamore Anderson had outlived her brother, her two nieces *and* a great-nephew. With the exception of the great-nephew, all had died from cardiac issues. Leitha herself had been ninety-three when her car went off the road this past spring. She had died as a result of her injuries. Researchers wanted to know why Leitha—and people like her—lived so long and were physically and mentally in such good shape. Was it genetics? Was it lifestyle? Was it both? Or neither? And was there any connection with other traits such as eye color or height?

Mike made a face. "Like I said, there were things she never talked about, and once she was gone, I was sorry I didn't push more. I felt this urgency to learn about the family while there were still people left to talk to." He held up a finger as though something had just occurred to him. "That reminds me, Kathleen: At some point I'd like to have a family tree drawn out. Isn't there a guy at the artists' co-op who does that sort of thing?"

"You're probably thinking about Ray Nightingale," I said.

Ray was best known for his intricate pen-and-ink drawings, which each featured a tiny fedora-wearing duck named Bo somewhere in the design. Ray had also drawn several family trees for different people—in one case drawing a very detailed actual tree to showcase that family's connections.

Mike snapped his fingers. "Nightingale. Right. That's the guy I was thinking of."

"I'm sorry. Ray isn't in town anymore." I held up one hand before he could speak. "But I know someone who should be able to help you." I gestured at Maggie, who was deep in conversation with Johnny. "Do you know Maggie Adams?"

"The yoga teacher?"

"Uh-huh. And she's also a very talented artist."

Mike had already started to nod. "Wait a second. Did she make that mannequin thing of Eddie a few years back for Winterfest?"

I nodded. "Yes, she did." The "mannequin thing of Eddie" had been responsible for Eddie and Roma ending up together.

"You think she could make what I'm looking for?"

"I do. But if she couldn't, or if she doesn't have time in her schedule, Maggie could put you in touch with another artist who could help you. She used to be the president of the artists' co-op."

"Fantastic," Mike said. "Introduce me."

We joined Maggie and Johnny and I made the introductions, explaining to Mags what Mike was looking for.

"Off the top of my head, I can come up with a couple of ways to go," she said. "You could go very minimalist, with a clean, simple design, and focus on the fonts and the paper. Or you could take the completely opposite tack and do something very detailed. What were you thinking of?"

I knew that gleam in her eye. She was interested.

Mike shrugged. "I don't know. Something more than just names on a piece of paper. Something that could be framed and hung on the wall."

"You know that all you're going to find in the family tree are brigands and reprobates," a voice said behind us.

I turned to find Jonas Quinn—Mike's cousin—and Jonas's nephew, Lachlan, grinning at us. I knew Jonas from the library. He was an avid reader of military history and "hard" science fiction and lately books on genetics, which made sense since Mike was digging into the family history. He was about the same height as Marcus, which meant he was just over six feet, and he had dark eyes and wavy dark hair cut much shorter than Mike's. Jonas was a college professor and Lachlan's guardian.

I knew Lachlan because he'd come to the library with Mike more than once. He was seventeen and a nice kid. He had the same thick hair as Mike and Jonas did, except his was long, pulled back into a ponytail. "A tangle of curls," I remembered Mary calling it.

"As you can probably tell, my cousin is not interested in our past," Mike said dryly.

"That's true." Jonas nudged his black brow-line glasses up his nose. "I'm looking to the future, which is Lachlan."

"Geez, no pressure," the teen said. I saw the gleam in his green eyes and knew he wasn't really feeling pressured.

"Lachlan wants to study music," Mike said.

"What's your dream school?" I asked.

Lachlan smiled. "Berklee," he said. "But I know how hard it is to get in, so I'm applying to other places as well. I want to be an audio engineer and music producer."

"He plays piano, guitar and bass," Jonas said.

I knew that Lachlan's father was Jonas Quinn's younger brother. Jonas had taken on raising the boy when his parents died as the result of a car accident. I could hear the parental pride in his voice.

"He's good," Johnny added. "I'm running out of things to teach him."

Lachlan ducked his head as a flush of color crept up his neck.

"I think you'd like Boston," I said as a way of changing the subject. "There's an incredible amount of music to see live. Whatever kind of music you like, someone somewhere in the city is playing it."

"That's where you grew up, right?" Lachlan asked.

I took a sip of my coffee. It had gotten cold. "For the most part. My family still lives there."

Maggie leaned into my line of vision. "Kath, you should connect him with Ethan," she said.

I nodded. "That's a good idea." I turned my attention to Lachlan again. "My younger brother, Ethan, is a musician. He could tell you all about the music scene in Boston, and a friend of his went to Berklee. Ethan teaches music and he has a band called The Flaming Gerbils."

Lachlan frowned. "Wait a sec. The lead singer? That's your brother? Ritchie played me a couple of their songs. They're really good. Man, I'd love to talk to him."

"Send me a text so I have your number and I'll pass it on to Ethan tomorrow," I said.

He pulled out his phone and I recited my number. He immediately sent me a text, then looked up smiling. "Seriously, thank you. There's so much stuff I'd like to ask him." The smile wavered. "You don't think he'll mind, do you?"

I laughed. "If Ethan's not making music, he's talking about music. He eats, sleeps and breathes it. He won't have any problem answering anything you ask him."

Maggie asked a question then about what other schools Lachlan was applying to. Watching him, I could see how much he resembled both Mike and Jonas. Like Mike he was very animated when he was talking, his hands flying everywhere, and he had the same way of tilting his head to the side while he was listening that Jonas did.

I pictured Ethan and Sarah, who didn't look that much alike even though they were twins, but who did share the same intensity about so many things. Ethan and I both had dark hair, but my eyes, like Sarah's, were brown and his were hazel. I felt a twinge of homesickness for my own family.

I could have stayed there talking all night. I saw Harry check his watch and Roma stifle a yawn.

Marcus came up behind me and put an arm around my shoulders. "Ready to go?" he asked.

I nodded. Across the room Johnny was at the counter getting the bill for his whole group, I realized. From the expression on Nic's face, he'd also added a very nice tip.

We gathered our things and said good night to Nic. Outside on the sidewalk I gave Roma a hug. "Thank you for suggesting this," I said, gesturing at the café behind us. "Best night ever."

"Absolutely," she said. She smiled, grabbed Eddie by the hand and they headed down the sidewalk.

Marcus was talking to Harry about something, their expressions serious. Maggie and Brady joined me. "Hey, thank you for suggesting me to Mike for his family tree," she said.

"So you're interested in designing it for him?" I asked.

She nodded. "I am. I got back into drawing when the bake-off was filming here and it's something I'd like to keep doing."

A failed attempt at resurrecting *The Great Northern Baking Showdown* had been filmed this past spring in Mayville Heights. Maggie had been hired to work with the show's illustrator.

"I can't wait to see what you come up with," I said. I turned to Brady. "A little bird told me your dad bought an air hockey table."

He gave his head a shake and smiled. "I'm guessing that bird's name is Rebecca."

"It is," I said.

"Doesn't surprise me," he said. "Rebecca is how Dad found out about it in the first place. She was at the office, they started talking and the next time I go out to the house, there's an air hockey table in the living room."

Rebecca was Rebecca Henderson. She was married to Everett Henderson. The office Brady had referred to was Everett's. Everett's assistant, Lita, and Brady's father, Burtis, were a couple. And to make things even more tangled, Rebecca and Everett were my backyard neighbors.

"I'll have to come out sometime for a game," I said.

"You know that's why he got the darn thing, don't you?" Brady said.

Brady had bought a pinball machine, which he kept out at his father's house. I was pretty good at pinball—as well as rod hockey, foosball and, yes, air hockey, the result of a lot of time spent hanging around while I was a kid and my parents did summer stock all up and down the East Coast. When I mentioned my skill at pinball, Burtis had challenged me to prove it. I had. More than once.

I grinned. "Tell Burtis I'll be happy to take his money anytime." The last time we'd played pinball, Burtis had suggested a small wager on the outcome of the game. Double or nothing had netted the Reading Buddies snack fund fifty dollars.

Marcus joined me then. We said good night to Maggie and Brady and headed for the truck.

"I don't think I'm ever going to forget tonight," I said as I unlocked the passenger door for Marcus.

"Johnny's going to do a couple of shows in Minneapolis next month," Marcus said as he climbed into the truck. "Why don't we try to catch one?"

"I'd like that." I slid behind the wheel. "Mike is trying to get the others to commit to doing a few of Johnny's shows with him."

Marcus smiled and fastened his seat belt. "So maybe we'll get to see Johnny and the Outlaws again."

I held up one hand, my middle and index fingers crossed. "Let's hope."

Marcus and I enjoyed a quiet Sunday. We had pancakes with Owen and Hercules, which should have meant that Marcus and I had pancakes and the cats had cat food, but in reality meant that Marcus and I had pancakes and he snuck (forbidden) bites to them and I pretended not to notice.

I called Ethan, who said he'd be happy to talk to Lachlan and promised he'd text right after we hung up. Then he spent ten minutes bombarding me with questions about the concert.

We walked down to the market at the community center after lunch and all anyone could talk about was the concert and the surprise reunion of Johnny and the Outlaws. I spotted Harrison Taylor Senior, Harry's father, with his lady friend,

Peggy. He was carrying a canvas shopping bag in one hand. Peggy smiled when she caught sight of me and I left Marcus at the Jam Lady's stall, trying to decide between strawberry-rhubarb jam and pear butter, and walked over to join them.

"Your son was amazing last night," I said, giving the old man a hug. He had thick white hair, a white beard that he kept cropped shorter in the summertime and deep blue eyes.

"Yes, he was," Harrison said, a huge smile splitting his face.

"Did you know?" I asked, raising an eyebrow at him.

"I knew something was up. All of a sudden the boy was never around." Harrison gave a snort of laughter. "To tell the truth, I thought he was seeing someone and didn't want me to know."

Harrison had been pushing his son—who had been divorced for years—to, as he put it, get a mitt and get back in the game. If Harry had met someone, he probably *would* be pretty closemouthed about it.

"I had no idea Harry was that good," I said. "I knew he'd been in a band but . . ." I shrugged.

"Harry's not the kind of person to blow his own horn," Peggy said with a smile.

Harrison set the shopping bag on the ground between his feet. "I remember when he got his first guitar and I'm kind of ashamed to say I told him it was a waste of money. He taught himself to play. Just sat there night after night in his room until the ends of his fingers cracked." He gave his head a little shake. "It's not a word of a lie. The dog wouldn't come in the house for six months. But that son of mine is stubborn."

"I wonder where that came from," Peggy said, almost under her breath.

Harrison shot her a look. "There's nothing wrong with my hearing, you know."

She leaned against his arm and smiled. "I know."

"Well, wherever his persistence came from, it paid off and I couldn't be prouder," the old man said. "I've been smiling since he started playin' and I don't think I'll be stopping anytime soon." His pride was evident in that smile and the sparkle in his blue eyes.

I spent a few more minutes catching up with Harrison and Peggy. Elizabeth, Harrison's youngest child, was coming for a visit in August and they were already planning a family barbecue.

"You're coming," he said. It wasn't a question. Harrison's definition of family was a wide one.

"I wouldn't miss it," I promised, standing on tiptoe to kiss his cheek.

I rejoined Marcus to discover that he'd bought the jam and the pear butter *and* a jar of the Jam Lady's marmalade, which was my favorite. We wandered around the market a while longer and then drove out to Marcus's house. I curled up on the swing on his back deck. Micah, Marcus's little ginger tabby, climbed up onto my lap, swatting me twice with her tail as she got settled. Marcus set up the ice cream maker for peach ice cream and grilled spicy sausage and corn on the barbecue. It had been pretty much the perfect weekend.

Monday morning I set out the census documents I'd told Mike about in our workroom so everything would be ready when he arrived in the afternoon. Considering their age and the fact that for a long time they'd been stuffed, forgotten, in an old filing cabinet in the library basement, the pages weren't in awful shape. Like the rest of our old documents, they would eventually be scanned and added to our digital database.

I relocked the workroom door and went into the staff room for a cup of coffee, taking it back to my office, where I stood by the window looking out at the gazebo. It was another beautiful day. Marcus was bringing lunch later and I thought how nice it would be to eat outside. It was good to see things looking quiet out there. In the spring the gazebo had been targeted by a practical joker who had—among other things—left an inflatable pool full of Jell-O in it. Black raspberry to be specific. It had been several weeks since the last stunt and I was hoping our prankster had gotten bored and moved on. Both Mary and Harry were convinced this was just a temporary respite from Jell-O, stacks of hay bales and a full-sized Grim Reaper with a broom instead of a scythe.

"Get it? It's the Grim Sweeper!" Susan, who had worked at the library long enough to have seen her share of stunts and pranks, had crowed with delight over that last one.

I was downstairs about an hour later, trying to fix a broken wheel on one of our book carts when Abigail called to me from the front desk.

"It's Marcus," she said, gesturing at the phone that I hadn't even heard ring.

"Thanks," I said as I got to my feet, brushing off the front of my flowered skirt. I walked over and picked up the receiver.

"Hi," Marcus said. He blew out a breath. "I'm not going to be able to make lunch." There was a flatness to his voice that told me he was in full police-detective mode.

"A case."

"Yes." He hesitated.

My stomach clutched. This was something bad.

"I'm sorry, Kathleen," he finally said. "There's no good way to say this. Mike Bishop is dead."

chapter 3

"No," I whispered. I closed my eyes for a moment and swallowed against the lump in my throat, which seemed to be stopping me from getting words out. "Are you . . . are you positive?"

"Yes. I wish I wasn't," Marcus said, "and I'm sorry but I have to go. I should make it for supper. I mean, if you still want to cook."

I nodded even though he couldn't see me. "I do." And because it suddenly seemed important, I added, "Stay safe."

"Always," he replied.

I hung up the phone and stood there, not moving, as Marcus's words began to sink in.

"Kathleen, what's wrong?" Abigail asked, coming around the side of the circulation desk. A frown creased her forehead and her eyes were narrowed in concern.

"It's, uh, it's Mike Bishop," I said slowly.

"What happened? Was he in some kind of accident?" She put a hand on my arm. Abigail had helped Mike with a lot of the research into his family tree. They'd gotten to be friends.

"I don't know what happened but . . ." I let the end of the sentence trail away. I didn't want to say the words out loud.

Abigail pressed her lips together and gave her head a little shake.

I swallowed again. It didn't seem to do anything for that lump in the back of my throat. "He's . . . dead."

A tear slid down her cheek and she swiped at it with one hand. "Are you sure?" she asked, looking away. "Maybe Marcus made a mistake. Maybe it was someone else."

I shook my head. "He doesn't make those kind of mistakes."

"I know," she said softly.

Neither one of us spoke for a moment. Then Abigail looked at me. "What do they give the dentist of the year?" she asked in a shaky voice.

I frowned at her, not really understanding the question. "I . . . I don't know."

"A little plaque." She laughed and then hiccupped. "Mike always had some awful dental joke to tell me when he came in and I'd always laugh because they were so bad." She wiped away another tear. "Why did the dental assistant refuse to date the dentist?"

I shook my head.

"He was already taking out a tooth."

I laughed then in spite of myself. "You're right," I said. "Those are terrible jokes."

"And remember how he hated it when someone called him a dentist?" Abigail asked. "Mary would do it just to tease him. He'd give her that look." She pushed her glasses down her nose and looked over the top of them at me. "And he'd say, 'Endodontist.' Then Mary would say something about how barbers used to do all that stuff *and* give you a shave and a haircut." She blinked away tears. "Oh, Kathleen, how can it be true?" Her shoulders sagged.

I didn't have an answer to her question. All I could do was give her a hug and blink back my own tears.

"You know Mike was genuinely excited about tracing his family tree," she said. "He told me that his cousin had warned him that he might find nothing but criminals and con men back there. He told me that he kind of hoped he would. That would be way more interesting than a family full of straitlaced rule followers."

"That sounds like Mike."

She gave me a small smile. "He looked like he was having so much fun being back onstage again. You could see it." She started to say something else and then stopped.

"What?" I asked.

"I was going to say that there's never going to be a night like that again, and then it hit me that now that Mike is . . . gone, there really isn't."

"We went to Eric's after the concert and they came in," I said. "Mike, Johnny, Harry—all of them. I told Mike about those census documents you found. He was coming in this afternoon to take a look at them. I set everything out in the workroom. I should go put things away again."

"I'll take care of it," Abigail said. "I mean, if it's all right with you. I could use a couple of minutes by myself."

"It's fine with me," I said. "Give me a minute to get Levi to keep an eye on the desk."

She nodded. "Thanks." She glanced over at the books she'd been sorting. "So Marcus didn't say anything about what happened? If it was a car accident or a heart attack."

"All he said was Mike was gone. He had to go and he didn't give me any details." I looked around for Levi, our summer student. "I'll be right back," I said.

I headed for the stacks where Levi was shelving books. The fact that Marcus *hadn't* said what had happened to Mike Bishop bothered me and I hoped Abigail hadn't noticed my discomfort at her question. He could have easily said Mike had had a heart attack or been in a car accident if either of those things had occurred. But he hadn't and I couldn't shake the feeling that something a lot worse had happened. I hoped I was wrong.

When the library closed for the day, I drove out to Marcus's house to make supper. Rebecca was checking in on Owen and Hercules, who I knew would be fine, but who were also more than a little spoiled. Marcus and I had talked about introducing his Micah to the boys. All three cats had been found out at Wisteria Hill—the old Henderson estate—and all three were far from typical cats, so I was hoping they'd get along.

Micah was waiting for me on the back deck. The little ginger tabby meowed hello and then jumped down to stand by the door and look expectantly at me. I let us both into the kitchen, set my bag on the table and dropped into one of the chairs.

Micah immediately launched herself onto my lap. She seemed to study me for a moment and then, as if sensing I was upset, she leaned her body against my chest with a soft "mrr." I stroked her fur and felt a little of the day's stress subsiding. The news about Mike had spread quickly and everyone who had come into the library seemed to want to talk about him. While it had been good to hear more stories about his sense of humor and quiet generosity, it had also been painful to realize that a good man was gone and wasn't coming back.

After a few minutes, I gave Micah one last scratch under her chin and set her on the floor. "Want to help me get supper?" I asked.

"Merow," she said, whiskers twitching.

That seemed to be a yes.

As I stood up, I realized that there were two physics text-books on the chair next to mine. I leaned down and opened the cover of the top book. It had come from the library in Minneapolis. There was a piece of paper poking out from between two pages just beyond the midpoint of the text.

These two books were the fifth and sixth books on theoretical physics Marcus had requested via interlibrary loan. Since he had found out about the special "skills" that Owen and Hercules *and* Micah had, he'd been looking for some sort of logical explanation. I'd struggled with telling him that all three cats had abilities that seemed to violate the laws of physics, at least as we knew them at this point in time. I'd put it off longer than I should have. I knew it had been hard for him to accept that Hercules had the ability to walk through any solid object, while both Owen and Micah could literally disappear at will—and usually at the most inconvenient times. Even when Marcus actually saw it happen, it was hard to believe it wasn't some kind of trick. I understood how he felt. It had taken me a little time to accept that I wasn't hallucinating, that I didn't have a brain tumor.

The first time I'd seen Owen disappear, I'd been able to convince myself it was just a trick of the light and my own overtired brain. When Hercules walked through a closed door after hours at the library, I'd thought that maybe I'd had a stroke. I had long suspected Micah had the same skill as Owen, so it wasn't as much of a surprise the first time she vanished, although the knowledge had come with the added worry that now I had to stop putting off telling Marcus just exactly how smart all three cats were.

I closed the cover of the book and straightened up. Micah was watching me, her head cocked to one side in curiosity. "He's persistent," I said.

"Mrr," she agreed.

I didn't think Marcus was going to give up until he found something that explained how the cats could do what they could do. That determined streak was one of the things that helped make him a good detective. Still, sometimes I thought he just needed to accept how things were and stop trying to find answers for questions that just might not have answers.

I washed my hands and set a pot of water on the stove to boil for the pasta. The cat watched and made little murping comments as I got out the rest of the ingredients for pasta salad.

"Should we eat in here or out on the deck?" I asked.

She immediately looked at the back door.

"Deck, it is," I said. "Excellent choice."

I moved the little round table Marcus kept out on the deck so it was in front of the swing and set it with place mats, napkins and silverware. While the pasta cooked, I put together a quick marinade for the chicken. Then I made the pasta salad, adding cucumber, celery, black olives and plump cherry tomatoes and radishes that Marcus had grown himself.

I'd just poured a glass of iced tea and stepped out onto the deck when Marcus came around the side of the house. "It's so good to see you," he said, wrapping his long arms around me and giving me a kiss.

"It's good to see you, too," I said. He looked tired. There was dark stubble on his chin, his pale yellow shirt was creased and I could see that he'd been raking his hands through his hair, something he did when he was stressed.

He reached up and brushed a stray bit of hair off my face. "Are you all right? I know the news about Mike was a shock."

"It's all anyone who came into the library was talking about. Do you know what happened yet?"

A shadow seemed to flit across his face. "Could I have a shower first?" He glanced over at the grill. "Do I have time?"

I nodded. "Go ahead. The salad's made and I'll start the chicken."

He blew out a breath. "Thanks," he said. He stopped to give Micah a scratch on the top of her head and went into the house.

The chicken was just about done when Marcus came out, wearing a pair of gray shorts and a red T-shirt, his hair damp from the shower. "Is that mine?" he asked, gesturing at the frosty glass of beer on the table.

"Yes, it is," I said. My iced tea was sitting to the left of the grill.

Micah was perched in the middle of the swing. "Get down," Marcus said, making a move-along gesture with one hand.

She wrinkled her whiskers at him and, instead of jumping

down, moved to the left and then looked at him. It seemed to me there was a challenge in her eyes.

Marcus shook his head. "Fine. Close enough," he said. He sat down next to the cat and reached over to stroke her fur.

I took the plate of chicken over to the table and joined them on the swing. "That smells great," Marcus said as he reached for the tongs I'd set on the table. "What did you put on the chicken?"

"Eddie's marinade and Harry's barbecue sauce," I said. I shook my head and sighed. Saying Harry's name made me realize how much he must be grieving right now.

Marcus put a hand on my shoulder. "I saw Harry a little while ago. He's okay. At least as okay as he can be under the circumstances."

"I can't believe Mike is dead," I said, dishing some of the salad onto my plate. "He was one of those people who just seemed so . . . alive." I looked at Marcus. "I know that doesn't make any sense."

"Yes, it does," he said.

I leaned back, balancing the plate on my lap as the swing began to gently move. "Marcus, what on earth happened? Mary said Mike died from a head injury. That doesn't sound like an accident."

Mary Lowe had come in to work at lunchtime. Her daughter, Bridget, was the publisher of the *Mayville Heights Chronicle*. Bridget always seemed to know the details of any police investigation long before they made any statements on a case.

Marcus swiped a hand over his face. "I don't know why I'm surprised to hear that," he said. "I swear, sometimes it seems like Bridget has the station bugged." Micah put a paw on his leg. He cut a sliver of chicken with the edge of his fork and gave it to her. She murped a thank-you. "It's way too soon for anyone to know the exact cause of death until the medical examiner finishes his work," he continued. "Bridget shouldn't speculate and spread rumors."

I noticed he hadn't said that what Mary had told me wasn't true. "Did someone break into his house?" I asked.

"Well, what's Bridget saying?" His voice was laced with sarcasm, which he seemed to realize the moment the words were out. "I'm sorry," he said. "It just . . . hasn't been a very good day."

I put my hand on his leg and gave it a squeeze. "I know," I said.

"At this point we don't know for certain what happened," he said after a brief silence. "Mike was found inside his house. If I had to guess, I'd say he died sometime Sunday night. Beyond that, I just don't know."

"Maybe it was an accident," I offered. "Maybe he tripped over something on the floor and hit his head. Maybe he had a seizure or a stroke."

"It's possible." Marcus didn't sound convinced.

"Could Mike have walked in on someone who broke into the house? I haven't heard of any break-ins in that area."

"There haven't been any. At least nothing that's been reported to us. I talked to Oren and the Kings. They haven't seen anything suspicious."

I folded one arm up over my head, my supper forgotten for the moment. "Do you think Mike was murdered?" I asked.

Marcus raked a hand back through his hair. "Don't ask me that, please," he said.

"Okay." I put a hand against his cheek for a moment. "Have something to eat," I said. "We don't have to talk about this right now."

He reached for the pasta salad and I picked up my fork even though my appetite was pretty much gone. I realized from the way Marcus had dodged my questions that he suspected Mike Bishop had been murdered. I had a familiar sinking feeling in my stomach.

It was the end of the week before the medical examiner declared Mike Bishop's death a homicide. For once the newspaper didn't offer any opinion on what had happened before the official ruling. Marcus had shown up with the news and a quart of mocha fudge ice cream. We were sitting in my two big Adirondack chairs in the backyard. Hercules was perched on the wide arm of my chair, washing his face and sneaking looks at my dish, while pretending he wasn't the slightest bit interested in what was in it. Owen was sitting at Marcus's feet. He knew his chance of getting even a tiny taste was slim to none and there was no chance it would be coming from me.

"The news will be in tomorrow's paper," I said. It wasn't a question. Bridget would have been looking for the story in Mike's death.

"I'll be surprised if it's not," Marcus said. He and Bridget had a cool, slightly prickly relationship. He and Mary, on the other hand, were friends. They seemed to have an unspoken agreement not to talk about Bridget.

"There's no way it could have been an accident?" I asked. It wasn't that I doubted the skills of the medical examiner. I just hated the idea that someone—anyone—had deliberately ended Mike Bishop's life.

Marcus was shaking his head before I got the words out. "I wish there was. I agree with the medical examiner, based on what I saw. Mike hit his head on the fireplace mantel and bled into his brain. Based on the location of the wound, there's no way it could have happened accidentally." His hand briefly touched the back of his head. "Between you and me, he was punched in the face right before he hit his head. I think he was moving away from the person who threw that punch. There was nothing on the floor he could have tripped over and nothing he could have slipped on."

Hercules looked at me, tipping his head to one side and narrowing his green eyes. "If Mike had tripped while he was moving away from whoever had hit him, wouldn't he have fallen forward, not backward?" I asked.

Hercules immediately looked at Marcus, as though he wanted to hear the answer to the question as well, as though

I'd asked what he'd wanted to know—which wasn't as unlikely as it seemed.

Marcus shrugged. "He could have been backing up."

"So Mike fought or struggled with some unknown person, and that person hit him and then pushed him or hit him again, which sent him into the mantel."

"That's one of the possibilities."

Hercules looked expectantly at me again. Was there something else he wanted to know? "But that suggests what happened wasn't premeditated, that it was most likely an accident. So why didn't that person call for help? It doesn't make any sense."

"I know. Mike Bishop was universally liked. I don't think you could find anyone in town—or in this part of the state for that matter—who had a bad word to say about the man."

"So why is he dead?" I said.

Marcus shrugged. "Right now I don't know."

It felt as though the entire town showed up for Mike Bishop's funeral on Saturday. That was one of the things I liked about living in a small town, this small town—everyone knew everyone else; everyone *cared* about everyone else.

It was more than four years now since I'd arrived in Mayville Heights. The head librarian position I'd come for was supposed to only be a temporary eighteen-month appointment, with the main part of the job being to supervise the refurbishment of the library in time for its centennial. I had applied on a whim, looking to get away from Boston after a relationship had fallen apart. The building had been beautifully restored, the collections had been reorganized and the computer system brought more or less into this century, but when the time was up, I found myself wanting to stay. I had Owen and Hercules. I had friends. I had a life I loved. I was lucky that the library board had wanted me to stay as well. As much as I sometimes missed my family back in Boston, Mayville Heights was my home now. Now I felt that sense of community very strongly.

Marcus and I sat with Eddie and Roma at the service. Roma had known Mike for years and she had taken his death hard. She had been pale but composed when she and Eddie pulled into Gunnerson's parking lot, but when I'd hugged her, she'd held on a little tighter and a little longer than usual.

I had closed the library an hour early because all of the staff wanted to attend the funeral.

"I was leaving one night after my shift and Mike asked me what I was listening to," Levi had said to me when he'd asked for the time off to attend the service. "I told him ZZ Top. About a week later, he comes in and says he has something for me. It was a concert T-shirt from the band's *El Loco* tour. I said I couldn't take it and he laughed. He patted his gut and said it didn't fit his needs anymore, and if I didn't wear it, the shirt would just sit in a drawer."

The service was being held at Gunnerson's Funeral Home.

Daniel Gunnerson Senior was at the front door, shaking hands and directing people. He was a short and solid man with deep blue eyes and a head of thick white hair. He wore a black suit with a crisp white shirt and a blue tie. The smaller rooms, which could accommodate several services, had been opened up to make one large space, and even so I wondered if there would be enough room for all the people I was expecting would come.

We took a seat about five rows back. Jonas and Lachlan were standing together at the front of the room with a bearded man I didn't recognize. Lachlan looked subdued. Jonas seemed even more serious than usual, his face pale. Their small family had gotten even smaller.

Roma looked around as though she was trying to find someone.

"What is it?" I whispered.

"I don't see Eloise," she said.

Eloise was the only other Finnamore cousin left. I'd met her when she'd come to town for her mother, Leitha's, funeral.

Marcus had heard our conversation and he leaned toward us. "She isn't coming. I spoke to her on Thursday. She had surgery on a broken leg a few days ago. She's not allowed to fly."

Roma nodded. "Thanks. I knew there had to be a good reason she wasn't here."

The man with the beard turned out to be a Unitarian minister and a college friend of Mike's. He led the service, sharing his own memories of Mike's sense of humor and his kind heart.

Jonas and Lachlan talked about how Mike had kept them together as a family. "He loved to cook, make music and bring people together," Jonas said. "He'd organize these Sunday meals, timed so that Eloise and the girls could join us from California over Zoom. We'd have dinner and they'd have lunch and the distance didn't matter because we were still all together like we'd been when we were kids."

I had to swallow back tears when Harry walked to the front of the room. He looked so somber in his dark suit. Roma was already holding Eddie's hand. She reached, wordlessly, for mine, squeezing it hard.

"Mike and I had been practicing for what turned out to be our last show for over a month," Harry said. "He loved the idea that we were going to surprise everyone. It was one of the best nights of his life, he told me after the concert. And according to Mike, he had a lot of those." Harry raised an eyebrow. A lot of people were smiling. Mike had been a charmer.

Harry let out a slow breath. "When someone dies, we always talk about what a great person they were when a lot of the time they were really a jerk, but Michael Bishop was not one of those people. Everyone loved him and he was a dentist. How many people love their dentist?"

"Endodontist," Lachlan called out.

Across the aisle from me, I saw Mary wipe away a tear.

Harry smiled and nodded his head. "Right. Endodontist."

He looked skyward. "Sorry, my friend." His expression grew serious again, and his gaze shifted to the pewter urn to the right of him under the photo of Mike playing his bass at the Last Bash concert. The polished container seemed too small to contain Mike's big personality. "The world was brighter with Mike Bishop in it and it's a little darker now that he's gone."

Johnny spoke last. "When Mike came to audition to join the Outlaws, he was dressed just like Sonny Crockett—Don Johnson—from the TV show *Miami Vice*: pleated pastel blue pants and a matching jacket with shoulder pads, a white T-shirt, loafers with no socks, shades and, because it was Mike, a mullet." He smiled at the memory. "I just knew from looking at him that he was the wrong fit for the band, so I asked him to play with Harry and do the bass line from Heart's 'Magic Man.' I figured there was no way he'd know the song. He was wearing a pastel suit for heaven's sake!"

There were a few ripples of laughter around the room.

"I was so sure he wouldn't be able to play it but he did and he played his part perfectly, in his own way, not a copy of anyone else. That was Mike."

Johnny had to pause for a moment and clear his throat. "People of a certain age will remember when Principal Haney canceled the senior class sleigh ride because he wasn't happy with the class average after Christmas exams. He got to school the next morning and his office was filled floor to ceiling with bales of hay." He glanced over at the urn and smiled. "He suspected Mike from the beginning but Mike had an alibi. He had spent the evening before calling bingo at the senior center like he did every Thursday night. Or so they all said."

There was more laughter.

"That was Mike."

Beside me Roma was nodding.

Johnny continued, "What most of you don't know is that when Mike was in college, he used to play stand-up bass for a Baptist church band, which meant he would be out playing at a bar with us until two a.m. and then he'd put on his white shirt, slick back his hair and be at the front of the church at nine thirty. He did that because the group's regular bass player—who also happened to be Mike's chemistry professor— was undergoing cancer treatment. That's also who Mike was."

He cleared his throat again. "Jonas and Lachlan asked us to sing something for Mike. We talked about it and we just couldn't sing anything that was sad because it just didn't feel right."

Harry and Paul had gotten to their feet. They joined Johnny while Ritchie moved to the piano set off to one side.

"Mike learned this one from those Baptists, and when he wanted to get under my skin, he'd start pushing to make it our encore. Please join us if you know the words." Johnny looked over at the urn one last time. "Safe travels, my friend." He clasped his hands in front of him and began to sing the poignant words of the old hymn "I'll Fly Away."

Jonas and Lachlan stood up and everyone else rose as well. One by one, throughout the room, I heard voices begin to join in. It was profoundly sad and somehow uplifting at the same time.

Outside, a fine, soft rain was falling. As I stood under the umbrella Marcus held over us and watched Daniel Gunnerson carefully set all that was left of Mike Bishop into the hearse, I thought of something I'd heard my mother say: *Blessed are the dead that the rain falls on.*

I hoped it was true.

chapter 4

The interment at the Finnamore family crypt was private and would be taking place at a later time. At the beginning of the service, Daniel Gunnerson had made an announcement that there would be a reception immediately after and most people did stay to pay their respects and talk about Mike.

"It seems like half the town is here," I said to Marcus. I was hoping to tell Harry how sorry I was but hadn't seen him since the service ended.

Everett Henderson joined us. "Kathleen, may I steal Marcus from you for a moment?" he asked. He was wearing a perfectly tailored black suit with a patterned gray silk tie that I knew Rebecca had bought for him because I'd been with her when she had.

"Of course," I said.

Marcus caught my hand and gave it a squeeze as he moved past me. "I'll only be a minute." He and Everett moved to a spot closer to the windows where there were fewer people.

I felt a hand touch my shoulder and turned around to find Harrison Taylor standing there. His suit was gray, his shirt and tie blue. He'd trimmed his hair and his beard. I hugged him.

"You look nice," I said. It struck me that Mike would get a kick out of everyone all dressed up. I'd only ever seen him in scrubs or jeans.

"Thank you," he said. "I wish it was for a better reason."

I nodded. "How's Harry?" I asked.

"Pretty much how you'd expect. It's a damn sad day." He ran a hand over his beard. "I know it's late notice, but I was hoping you could come for supper tomorrow night."

"I could," I said. Marcus and I didn't have any plans. A couple of Eddie's hockey buddies from his NHL days were coming to spend a few days teaching at the hockey school and Eddie had invited Marcus to join them for dinner. "I don't want to put Harry out, though." Generally, when I had dinner with Harrison, it was his son who did most of the cooking.

"You won't be," the old man said.

I suspected he was going to ask me to see what I could learn about Mike Bishop's death. I'd gotten involved in that kind of thing before. People were more likely to talk to me than they were to the police. In that way being a librarian was a lot like being a bartender, I'd discovered.

We settled on a time and then Harrison excused himself to go speak to Daniel Gunnerson. I turned around to look for Marcus, and Jonas Quinn caught my eye. He held up one hand, indicating that he wanted to talk to me. He said something to Lachlan, who was standing next to him, and then started across the room.

"Kathleen, thank you for coming," he said as he joined me.

"I'm so sorry," I said. "Mike was a good person. I'm glad I got to know him."

Jonas nodded. "Yes, he was. Him being dead is just so wrong and it should never have happened." He looked around. "You know, he would have liked this, all these people here in one place talking about him."

I smiled. "Mike was a people person. He'd come into the library and it would take him half an hour to get started on his research because he knew everyone and he kept stopping to talk."

"That research is why I wanted to talk to you," Jonas said. He adjusted his dark-framed glasses with both hands. "The last time I spoke to him, Mike mentioned that you had unearthed more information about the Finnamore family."

"Some census information for this area," I said. "Mike was trying to close a gap in the family tree. I thought it might help."

"Would it be possible to get a copy of it?" he asked. "I think Mike's research on the family is something Lachlan—and maybe Eloise for that matter—might want at some point. Not just because it's their family heritage, but because it was something Mike was working on. I don't want everything to get lost in the shuffle. There's a lot to take care of right now."

"I understand," I said. "I can make copies of the census records for you and you can come in next week and get them. There's also a copy of a map showing land grants for this part of the state that's coming from another library in our system. Would you like that as well?"

He nodded. "Yes, I would."

I told Jonas I'd call when the map arrived so he could make just one trip to pick up everything.

He thanked me again. "I need to get back to Lachlan," he said. "I'll talk to you soon."

I watched him make his way over to his nephew and put one arm around the boy's shoulders. I knew from some of the things Mike had talked about that there was a lot of tragedy in the Finnamore family history. I hated that Mike himself was now part of that.

I looked for Marcus. He was still talking to Everett. I was guessing their conversation had something to do with the girls' hockey team. There had been rumblings that their funding might be reduced.

The room suddenly felt closed in and clammy. I was only a

few steps away from a set of French doors that led out to the overflow parking lot. No one would notice if I stepped outside, so that was what I did.

The rain had stopped. The air was fresh and a little cooler. I remembered that there was a teak bench next to a small flower bed at the end of the building. I'd sit there for a couple of minutes and then go back inside, I decided.

I turned the corner to discover someone was already sitting on the bench. And she was crying.

She looked up at me. Her eyes were red and her makeup had smudged. I pulled a couple of tissues from my bag and handed them to her. She wiped her face. "Thank you," she said in a shaky voice.

"Can I get you anything?" I asked. "A cup of tea, maybe?"

She shook her head. "I don't think I could swallow it."

"I know what you mean," I said. "I was carrying around a cup inside just so people would stop offering me a drink."

She almost managed a smile. "You must have been a friend of Mike's."

I nodded. "I like to think so. I'm Kathleen Paulson."

"You're the librarian. Mike mentioned you. He said you'd been helping him with the family tree."

I nodded.

"I'm Tracy," she said. "I'm Mike's ex-wife." She held up a finger. "The first one."

"It's nice to meet you," I said.

She moved sideways on the bench. "Please, sit."

"I didn't mean to intrude."

She shook her head. "You're not. I was in there listening to people talk about him and I thought what a kick he'd get out of this—everyone dressed up, sharing stories. You know, I think the only time I ever saw him in a suit was actually at a funeral."

She'd had just the same thought as me. "You didn't have a fancy wedding?" I asked.

Tracy's lips twitched. She seemed to think my question was funny. Mirth gleamed in her dark eyes. It was better than sadness. "Good grief, no!" she said. "We were nineteen and madly in love. We eloped. Turns out, we were really just madly in lust. The marriage didn't last six months but the friendship did."

"That sounds like the Mike I knew."

"Every few months he'd call me or I'd call him, just to catch up. It was nice, having that connection back to when I was a dumb kid." She smiled. "I just talked to him a couple of weeks ago. He told me all about the research he was doing into his family's past. He was trying to work out when the so-called Finnamore green eyes entered the family tree. I teach high school biology. I told him he was wasting his time. There are too many factors that influence eye color. It's not as simple as something like hair texture or whether or not someone thinks cilantro tastes like soap."

"It does," I said.

She nodded. "I know."

We sat in silence for a moment. "I'm going to miss talking to him," she finally said.

I reached over and gave her hand a quick squeeze. "I should get back inside."

"Me too," Tracy said. "It was very nice to meet you."

"You too," I said.

"Do you want to go over to Fern's for supper?" Marcus asked as we pulled out of the parking lot about half an hour later. The sky was low and gray and it was raining again. He was dropping me off and then going in to the station for a little while. "A case that's coming up in court soon," he'd offered by way of explanation.

"I have spaghetti sauce," I said.

He shot me a quick sideways glance. "Does one somehow negate the other?"

I shook my head. "No. I can have it tomorrow— Wait. I can't. I'll eat it Monday."

"Is there some rule that says you can't eat spaghetti on Sundays because I'm pretty sure I've broken it more than once?"

I smiled. "No, there isn't. It's just that I'm going out to have supper with Harrison tomorrow."

Marcus didn't say anything for a moment and he kept his eyes fixed to the road. I let the silence sit between us. "You know why he invited you," he finally said.

"Yes," I said. "He likes my company."

"He thinks you can figure out who killed Mike Bishop."

"He probably does."

"What are you going to say?"

I looked over at him. His blue eyes were still looking straight ahead. "I don't know," I said.

And I didn't. I adored Harrison. I considered Harry a friend. I wanted to help them if I could. This wasn't the first time I'd gotten mixed up with one of Marcus's case, so I wasn't sure why I was so uncertain. Why this time felt different. Maybe it was because Mike and I were friends or close to it. His death felt so personal. I wasn't sure I could be objective.

Marcus sighed softly. "I'm not going to tell you what to do, Kathleen."

I reached over and touched his arm. "I appreciate that."

"But I am going to *ask* you to think carefully about whatever choice you make. This case is deeply personal for a lot of people, including you and me. It's harder to be objective. It's harder to set your own feelings to one side. It's harder not to pick up other people's pain." He glanced briefly at me then. "That last part you're going to have to deal with no matter whether you say yes or no to Harrison."

We were at the house by then. Marcus pulled into the driveway and put the SUV in park. I undid my seat belt, leaned over and kissed his cheek. "I promise I'll think carefully about whatever choice I make," I said.

"I know you will." He kissed the side of my mouth and smiled at me. "You didn't give me a yes or no about Fern's."

"Yes." Fern's meat loaf and mashed potatoes were the ultimate comfort food and that sounded pretty good right about now.

"I'll call when I'm leaving," Marcus said. He kissed me a second time.

I got out, opened my umbrella and watched him back out of the driveway before I headed around the side of the house to the back door. Hercules was sitting on the bench in the sun porch. He made a face as I held my half-open umbrella out the door and gave it a shake. I propped it in the corner and sat down next to him.

"Mrr," he said, cocking his head to one side almost as though he was asking if I was okay.

"I'm all right," I said, kicking off my shoes. "It was a nice service. Very sad."

Hercules moved closer, putting his two front paws on my leg. I stroked his fur. I had no idea how much of what I said to them either cat understood—a lot more than the average cat, I was certain. Given what else they could do, it didn't seem that implausible.

"I think Harrison is going to ask me to try to figure out who killed Mike Bishop." The cat wrinkled his nose at me as though considering what I'd just said.

Hercules and I had been listening to whatever songs by Johnny and the Outlaws I could find online. Even Owen seemed to like the band's music. He didn't always share my taste in music the way Hercules did. Whenever I had gotten involved in one of Marcus's cases, so had the boys, as far-fetched as that seemed. More than once, Owen's ability to disappear and Herc's to walk through walls had helped me learn something I wouldn't otherwise have figured out. I hadn't been able to convince Marcus of that, though.

Hercules seemed to have come to some sort of conclusion. He jumped down from the bench and went into the kitchen without waiting for me to unlock the back door. I sighed, picked up my shoes and followed him, stopping to open the door first. Hercules was already halfway across the kitchen, headed for the living room. He was a cat with a purpose. I had no idea what he was up to.

He made his way across the room and launched himself into the big wing chair. I folded my arms and glared at him. "Excuse me. That's a people seat not a cat seat," I said.

His response was to stare pointedly at my laptop, which was sitting on the footstool.

I shook my head. "No."

Hercules looked over at me and blinked his green eyes a couple of times.

"Yes, I get that you think I should say yes to Harrison," I said.

He continued to look at me.

"I'm still thinking about it."

Hercules was as motionless as a statue. I knew better than to get into a staring contest with him. I wouldn't win.

"I need to get out of these clothes first *and* I'd like a cup of coffee," I said.

He meowed softly and began to wash his face. It was easy to be magnanimous when you'd won, especially when you were a cat.

I put the laptop on the kitchen table, started the coffeepot, then went upstairs and changed into a red-striped T-shirt dress that was comfortable for sitting around in but would also be okay to wear to Fern's later.

I had just poured my coffee when Hercules poked his head around the living room doorway and meowed inquiringly at me.

"I'm ready," I said. I snagged the nearest chair with one foot, pulled it closer and sat down. The cat padded over to the table and launched himself onto my lap.

"So what should we look for?" I asked. I talked to Hercules and his brother, Owen, a lot. Saying out loud what was running through my mind helped me make sense of things. At least that was how I rationalized it.

Hercules gave me a blank look. Okay, it seemed where to start was my department.

"By the way, where's your brother?"

"Mrr," he said with what looked to me like a shrug.

Translation: *I don't know.*

Given the fact that Owen could become invisible anytime he wanted to, it was possible he was here in the kitchen right now. Possible but not very likely. Owen was very good at disappearing. Hiding the fact that he was "hiding," not so much. My guess was that he was either in his basement "lair," where

70

he stashed things he'd swiped from around the house, or up-stairs on the bed in the spare room—somewhere he knew he wasn't supposed to be.

"Maybe we should poke around on social media," I said to Hercules. "If Mike surprised someone who had broken into his house, maybe it wasn't the first time they'd done something like that. Marcus said there hadn't been any break-ins reported, but people don't always call the police if nothing's been stolen." I raised an eyebrow at him. "What do you think?"

"Merow!" he said. Hercules was almost always enthusiastic about helping me do some online research. He'd peer at the screen and move his head as though he were reading an article or checking out a photograph. Oddly enough, more than once, a seemingly stray tap of his paw at the keyboard had landed me on just the piece of information I was looking for.

I thought about who lived in the same area as Mike had, working my way along the closest streets in my mind. Just about everyone used some form of social media, it seemed. A lot of people were talking about Mike's death and about the reunion of Johnny and the Outlaws. I couldn't find any mention of any break-ins in the area.

Hercules stayed perched on my lap, green eyes glued to the laptop screen, one paw on the table edge. When I leaned back and reached for my coffee, he tapped a paw on the touch pad, then turned and looked at me.

"Okay, what did you do?" I asked, leaning around him so I could see the screen.

He looked from the computer to me. If he could have raised an eyebrow and said, *Duh*, he probably would have.

We seemed to have somehow landed on the Facebook page for Keith King's storage business. I'd seen Keith a lot more frequently at the library in the past few months. He was one of the newest members of the library board, and like Mike, he had been researching his family history after receiving one of those DNA test kits.

I read a few of his posts but didn't find anything useful. I was about to give up and move on when I spotted it. About three weeks ago, Keith had offered a deal on renting a medium-sized storage unit: rent for twelve months and get one month free. *Keep your snowblower and winter gear safe from anyone with sticky fingers who might walk through your yard.*

I leaned back in the chair, putting one hand on Hercules so I wouldn't knock him off my lap.

"That could just be a promotional line," I said. "It doesn't mean there's been someone wandering around people's yards out where Keith lives."

"Mrr," Hercules said without moving his gaze from the laptop's screen.

"Yes, I know. It doesn't mean there hasn't been, either." I could call Keith, but I wasn't sure how to ask him without explaining why I wanted to know.

I looked at the computer again. There were comments under Keith's post, I noticed. I scrolled through them slowly. The third-to-the-last one gave me what I was looking for. It had been made by one of the Reading Buddies moms. She had jokingly asked if Keith had a unit large enough for her car because she'd had some change and a set of AirPods swiped from it while the family was on their back deck eating supper. Another commenter had commiserated with her, saying that unfortunately you had to keep your car locked all the time these days, even in Mayville Heights. Someone had sprayed whipped cream all over her front and back car windows.

It wasn't exactly a smoking gun, and there was a big difference between grabbing a pair of AirPods from an unlocked car and killing a man in his own living room. Still, I couldn't help thinking that I might be onto something. At the same time, I was uncomfortably aware that I was already digging into a murder I wasn't sure I wanted to get involved in—or even should.

chapter 5

Marcus picked me up just before six and we drove over to Fern's. It seemed I wasn't the only one who was looking for comfort food. The diner was busy but I was glad Marcus had suggested we eat out. It had been such a sad day, I was glad to be around other people.

Peggy was just coming out of the kitchen when we walked into the diner. She was still wearing the navy dress she had worn to Mike's service. She smiled, grabbed a couple of menus and showed us to a booth by the windows.

"How's Harrison?" I asked Peggy. "He didn't find the service too much?"

"I asked him that very question and he said he's not feeble

yet, thank you very much." She shook her head. "That man is stubborn to the bone. On the other hand, it's a quality he passed down to all three of his children. I told him that was karma in action."

I smiled. Larry was actually the most easygoing of all the Taylors. Harry, and especially Elizabeth, were just like their father.

"I almost forgot," Peggy said. "Eugenie says hello."

Eugenie Bowles-Hamilton was a cookbook author who owned a very popular bakery in Vancouver, Canada. We'd met when the revival of the *Great Northern Baking Showdown* was filming in Mayville Heights back in the spring. Eugenie was one of the two cohosts of the show, straight woman to Russell Perry, the lead singer for The Flying Wallbangers. I'd been hired, part-time, to research and provide background information for the hosts—primarily Eugenie—that fit with whatever each particular week's focus happened to be.

"You were talking to her?" I asked.

"I saw her in person. I was in Chicago for a couple of days last week to film a small part on another baking show."

"That's wonderful," I said.

Peggy had ended up stepping in at the last minute for one of the baking showdown's judges. She turned out to be great on camera, and even though the show ended up not airing, word of her warm personality and rapport with the other judge and the contestants had gotten around.

"Would you believe Richard suggested me?" she asked.

Richard Kent had been the other judge on the *Great Northern Baking Showdown*.

I nodded. "I would. The two of you had great chemistry."

"We work well together, and while I don't want to make a career out of this, it was more fun to be back in front of the camera than I'd expected." She smiled. "Your waiter will be right over."

After we'd given the waiter our orders, I spotted Mariah Taylor, Harry's daughter, clearing two booths at the far end of the diner. She was working at Fern's part-time for the summer and helping her father as well.

"I just want to go speak to Mariah for a second," I said to Marcus. "I'll be right back."

It had occurred to me that swiping a set of AirPods and spraying whipped cream all over someone's windshield sounded like the kinds of things a group of teenagers might do.

Mariah was stacking glasses in a large plastic bin. She noticed me and smiled. "Hey, Kathleen," she said.

"How's the job going?" I asked.

"Don't tell my dad, but I think I like working for him a lot better." She gestured at the table. "People are pigs sometimes."

"I know," I said. "I had this same job when I was your age. How many times have you found gum stuck to the back of a booth?"

She made a face. "Twice. One time I put my hand on it."

I nodded in sympathy. "I kneeled on a big wad of grape bubble gum once."

Mariah brushed a stray strand of hair back off her face. "This is where you're supposed to tell me to stay in school so I won't have to clear tables for the rest of my life."

I smiled. "First of all, there are worse jobs than this, and second, you're smart enough to know the value of staying in school."

"Yeah, well, could you tell my dad that last part?" Mariah said.

I laughed. "Bugging you about that kind of thing is part of his job description."

That got a smile out of her.

"Mariah, do you know anything about some cars being vandalized out near where you live?"

She flushed and her gaze slipped away from mine. "Sorry. I don't."

I tipped my head to one side and studied her. "You're a crappy liar, you know."

She stared down at the table for a moment. "You can't tell my dad."

"As long as you're not doing anything dangerous," I said.

Mariah shook her head. "I wasn't doing anything dangerous and it was a onetime thing, believe me."

I nodded. "Okay. What did you do?"

She dropped her gaze again. "I went to this party with a girl from my class. There was a lot of drinking and I heard a couple of other girls talking about spraying whipped cream all over someone's car because the owner had complained about this dog getting loose and doing you know what all over her flowers."

"Did you know the girls?"

Mariah looked at me then. "One is a year behind me and I didn't know the other one." She blew the stray hair off her face again. "The whole thing turned out to be a stupid waste of time. The girl I went with hooked up with some summer guy and ditched me and I didn't have any way to get home."

"But you did get home okay?" I asked. I thought about how many times Ethan and Sarah had done something like that and then called me so Mom and Dad wouldn't find out. Not that I'd ever thought Mom and Dad were that oblivious.

"Yeah," she said, dropping a handful of forks into her bin. "I called Peggy and she rescued me. And she didn't rat me out to Dad. And before you say I could have called him, Peggy already said that."

I struggled to keep from smiling. "She's right you know," I said. "And you can always call me if you get into another situation like that."

"Really?"

"Really."

She smiled. "Thank you," she said. She looked over at Marcus. "You want me to tell him all of this?"

"Just the part about the whipped cream and the dog."

"Okay." She dipped her head in the direction of the booth. "You'd better go. Your food is ready."

On Sunday, Marcus and I decided to go to the flea market out on the highway. I had been making a halfhearted effort to find a couple of Adirondack chairs for his backyard.

"What about those benches instead?" he asked, pointing at a pair at a stall just up ahead.

"Maybe," I said. "Or maybe benches and a pair of Adirondacks."

He laughed. "You're not going to give up on those chairs, are you?"

"The arms are perfect for holding a glass of lemonade or a cup of coffee."

"Or a cat," Marcus said with a grin.

I smiled back at him. "That too."

We walked over to check out the benches and discovered that Burtis and Lita were doing the same thing. Burtis and Lita seemed like an unlikely couple on paper. He was rough-and-tumble and as a young man had worked for the town bootlegger. Lita had been Everett Henderson's right hand for as long as anyone could remember. I had no idea how Burtis and Lita had gotten together—as far as I knew, no one did—but they were good for each other and the way they sometimes looked at each other made my heart happy.

"You thinking of buying those for your backyard?" Burtis said to me.

I tipped my head toward Marcus, who was already walking

around one of the benches, checking it out. "Marcus's yard," I said.

The ends of the bench were cast iron and the back and the seat were made of wood. Both pieces looked to be in good shape. The only issue was the fact that all the wood on both pieces had been painted a vibrant fluorescent orange, the same shade as a highway safety sign.

"I'm thinking that with a little elbow grease and some paint they'd look pretty good in my backyard," Brady's father said. He was strong and solid with thick, muscular arms and a face lined and weathered from so much time spent outdoors. Burtis had lost most of his hair, just a few white tufts poked out from under his ubiquitous Twins ball cap.

Marcus tipped the bench forward with one hand so he could look at the underside of the seat. "Funny. I was thinking the same thing," he said.

"You should show a little respect for your elders and let me have them," Burtis said.

Marcus gave a snort of laughter as he set the bench down. "You're far from old. Nice try, though."

Burtis pointed a finger at him. "That sounds like something your father would say."

"I take that as a compliment," Marcus said.

Burtis smiled. "How is the old man?" he asked. Burtis and Marcus's father, Elliot, had been friends from the time they were teenagers.

"He's good. I talked to him a couple of nights ago. He says he's coming for a visit in a couple of weeks."

"Let me know if Elly May commits to a time," Burtis said. "We haven't been on a tear in a while." He grinned.

Lita shook her head. "One of us had better have bail money," she said to me.

I laughed. The last time Elliot Gordon had been in town, he and Burtis had taken a walk down memory lane with a few too many Jäger Bombs. The evening had ended with them serenading patrons in the lounge at the St. James Hotel with their version of "Sweet Home Alabama." The crowd had actually seemed to enjoy the music. Management, not so much.

Burtis and Marcus were haggling about the benches now.

"I saw the two of you at the service," Lita said. "Mike and I are . . . were cousins about four times removed."

Lita was related in one way or another to pretty much everyone in Mayville Heights. Her mother's family and her father's family were among the first non–Native American settlers in the area. As Rebecca had once explained it to me, "Half the town is cousin to Lita on her father's side and the other half is related through her mother."

"So you're connected to the Finnamores?" I asked.

She nodded. "If you go back far enough, some of the branches of our family trees intertwine." She glanced over at the men still debating who should get the benches. "Does Marcus have any suspects yet?"

I shook my head. "He wouldn't tell me if he did, but I don't think so."

"I hate the thought that someone broke into the house to rob it and then killed Mike. We like to think something like that would only happen in a big city, not in Mayville Heights, but past events show that's not true."

She gave me a knowing look, probably because I'd gotten tied up in more than one suspicious death since I'd arrived in town. I let it pass without comment.

"It's almost like that family is cursed."

"What do you mean?" I asked.

"It's only been a few months since Leitha died."

I remembered how Mike had explained that the older woman was his great-aunt the first time he'd come into the library to start digging into the family's history.

"The Finnamores tend to die too soon," she continued. "That's why there's so little of the family left now. Leitha hated that there were so few children. She was proud of being a Finnamore. The thought that the line could die out gave her a lot of grief."

"She always introduced herself as Leitha Finnamore Anderson," I said.

"She claimed the Finnamores could trace their ancestry back to the *Mayflower.*"

I nodded. "I'm not giving away any secrets because Mike was telling everyone. It appears from what he unearthed that

that much is true, but instead of being on the ship for religious reasons, it seemed their ancestor was in fact just a hired hand who eventually ended up with a family in England and one here in the colonies."

Lita gave a wry smile. "That would have burned Leitha's biscuits if she'd known. That family line meant everything to her. She hated that Mike had been married and divorced twice and hadn't had any children. He used to try to get a rise out of her by saying he didn't have any kids that he knew of."

That sounded like Mike. "And Jonas has no children, either," I said.

"Well, Jonas is not a biological Finnamore," Lita said. "He's the child of Nathan St. James Quinn from his first marriage, although Mary-Margaret Finnamore Quinn was his mother in every way."

"St. James like the hotel?"

Lita nodded. "Yes. Nathan's family owned it for years until it was sold. The family built the hotel." She glanced over at Marcus and Burtis, who still seemed to be debating who was going to end up with the benches.

"This is going to be a while," Lita said. "There's a guy at the end of this row selling donuts. I'm going to go get half a dozen. Do you want to come with me?"

"Absolutely," I said.

The donuts were cinnamon spice, with and without sugar. I got half a dozen to take to work with me on Monday. When

Lita and I got back, Marcus and Burtis were each buying one of the benches from the owner of the stall.

I smiled at Lita. "As Shakespeare would say, 'All's well that ends well.'"

We managed to get the bench onto the truck, off the truck and around into the backyard with a little physics (me) and a lot of muscle (Marcus). Those cast-iron ends were much heavier than I'd expected. Micah jumped up on the slatted seat, seemed to frown at the garish color and then, after she'd sniffed it and walked the length of the bench, meowed her approval.

I headed out to Harrison's for supper a couple of hours later, taking along some tomatoes from my garden and some cheese-and-ham biscuits that Rebecca had given me the recipe for. The old man lived in a small house on his son's property. He must have been watching for me because he and Boris, his dog, were standing at the door when I climbed out of the truck. Boris, with his chocolate velvet eyes, came over to meet me. I bent down to talk to him before walking over to join Harrison. I knew no matter how well I washed my hands when I got home, the cats would smell Boris on me and I'd be in the dog-house, so to speak. The dog actually belonged to Harry but spent a lot of time with Harrison. He was gentle and quiet and

I didn't like to think about what one of them would do without the other.

"I'm glad you made it," Harrison said.

"I'm glad you invited me." I gave him a hug and handed over the tomatoes and biscuits.

"Which are these?" he asked, eyeing the container of cherry tomatoes.

I'd been growing several varieties of heirloom tomatoes this year, letting Harrison try each one.

"These are sungold," I said. "They have a lovely sweet flavor. There are way, way more of them than I expected. And the biscuits are ham and cheese." I smiled. "Rebecca's mother's recipe."

He smiled. "Thank you. This will be my lunch tomorrow. Or maybe my breakfast. A man can eat only so much oatmeal and flaxseeds." I knew Peggy had been trying to get Harrison to eat healthier. He grumbled about it, but she'd had more success than his sons or Elizabeth.

We moved inside, Boris leading the way.

"We're dining alfresco," Harrison said.

"Does that mean I get to see the screened porch?" I asked. Harry and his younger brother, Larry, had been working on the addition to the house in their spare time.

The old man smiled and nodded. "You're my first guest."

I smiled back at him. "I'm honored."

We moved through the house to the screened porch at the

back. It was beautifully built—no surprise. The boys had their father's talent for carpentry. A set of wide steps led down to a small stone patio and Harry was there at the grill. He raised a hand in hello and I waved back.

"When he heard you were coming out, he insisted on grilling and you know what my boy's like when he makes up his mind," Harrison said.

"I have a little experience with the Taylor family stubbornness."

His blue eyes twinkled. "Are you suggesting he gets that from me?"

"Apples and trees, Harrison," I said. "Apples and trees."

There was a small table set for three. I knew Harry often ate with his dad when his kids were off with their friends or their mother, his ex-wife. I was glad he was joining us. I also knew there was a possibility I'd get tag-teamed by the two of them about Mike Bishop's death.

Harrison pointed to a couple of wicker chairs with deep green seats and back cushions. "Have a seat," he said. "Peggy picked those chairs, so I promise you they're comfortable. She said the two I wanted to use out here were older than Moses."

The chair was very comfortable. Maybe a couple of them would work in Marcus's backyard. I made a mental note to ask Peggy about them. Boris came over, leaned against my leg and set his head in my lap.

Harrison frowned at the dog. "Just give him a push," he said to me as he sat down in the other chair.

"He's fine," I said, reaching to scratch behind Boris's left ear. "He can sit by me whenever he wants." As if he'd understood my words, the dog turned to look at the old man as if to gloat.

"You're spoiled," he told the dog. Boris closed his eyes and gave a contented sigh.

"What's been going on at the library?" Harrison asked.

He was going to wait until after we'd eaten to talk about Mike Bishop, I realized, assuming I was right about why I'd been invited for supper.

I told him about the Summer Reading Club, the plans for a Money Week in the fall and about the library participating in World Mental Health Day in October.

"Sounds like you're keeping busy," he said.

I grinned at him. "It keeps me out of trouble. Tell me more about Elizabeth. You said she's coming next month?"

He nodded. "Before she goes back to college. It's taken a while for her to find her niche, but she's been making noise about medical school or biomedical engineering. I'm hoping one of those sticks. I have to say I'd love to have a doctor in the family."

I could hear the pride in his voice. Elizabeth had been placed for adoption when she was born. Harrison and her biological mother had had a relationship when Harrison's wife was in a nursing home, something he still carried some shame about. It had taken some time for the two of them to get to know each other, but he had answered every question she'd had without dodging the messy ones and that had gone a long way to helping them build a close relationship.

Harry came in from outside then.

"You did a wonderful job on this porch," I said, gesturing with one hand.

"Thanks," he said. He cleared his throat. "I saw you and Marcus at the service. I wanted to thank you both for coming. I'm sorry I didn't get a chance to talk to you there."

"I liked Mike," I said. "I wish I'd had the time to get to know him better. He'd come in to work on the family tree, and first thing I knew, he'd be in one of the meeting rooms charming the seniors."

Harry laughed. "That sounds like him."

"What can I do to help?" I asked.

Before Harry could answer, his father spoke up. "You're a guest and you don't have to work for your supper."

Harry smiled. "Thank you for the offer, Kathleen, but I have everything under control. We'll eat in about five minutes."

As usual, the food was delicious: barbecued steak, chopped salad and sourdough bread. I recognized the bread as Rebecca's honey-sunny recipe. Harry confirmed that I was right.

"Peggy made it," he said.

"I'll remember to thank her next time I see her," I said.

During supper we talked about Harry's garden—his cucumbers were doing better than mine—and the fact that the prankster who had been leaving things in the library's gazebo seemed to have given up.

"Whoever it is will be back. You just watch," Harry said.

"Mary certainly agrees with you," I said. "I'm hoping that finding the camera that you and Larry put up might have made whoever has been pulling these stunts realize this whole thing really isn't funny."

Harry just shrugged. "We'll see."

For dessert there was orange-banana frozen yogurt that the old man had made in his son's ice cream maker.

"This is so good," I exclaimed. I fought the urge to use my finger to get the last creamy bit out of my bowl. The yogurt was the perfect combination of citrus and sweet.

"I still have a few tricks left up my sleeve," Harrison said with a mischievous grin.

Harry rolled his eyes. "And that's what worries me."

Harrison still had the grin. "You need to blow a little of the carbon out of your spark plugs, if you get my drift." He had a naughty-boy gleam in his blue eyes and I thought once again what a charmer he must have been when he was a young man. He was certainly charming enough now.

"And on that note." Harry got to his feet. He gathered our bowls. "I have a couple of things to do."

"Thank you for supper," I said.

He smiled. "You're welcome here anytime. It's the least I can do since you keep my father in muffins and reading material."

Boris was sitting next to my chair. Harry patted his leg. "Let's go," he said to the dog.

"Leave him be," Harrison said. "I'll bring him over later."

Harry gave his head a little shake. "All right," he said. "Don't feed him any of that frozen yogurt." He headed into the house.

"Do you want to stay out here or move inside?" I asked Harrison.

"There's a nice breeze coming in through those screens and no bugs," he said. "Are you up for staying out here?"

"Absolutely," I said.

We moved over into Peggy's new chairs. I looked out over the back of Harry's property. "This is a beautiful spot," I said.

"That it is," he agreed. He stroked his beard with his thumb and index finger.

I turned and looked at him, narrowing my eyes.

"I know that look," he said. "You think I had an ulterior motive for inviting you out here."

"Didn't you?" I countered. "You want me to dig into Mike Bishop's death."

"I wouldn't want to risk our friendship by asking you to do that and putting you in a bad spot with Detective Gordon." He actually managed a little self-righteousness in his tone.

I got up and went over to hug him. "Because if I'm a true and loyal friend, I'll do it without you asking me. Am I right?"

He laughed and I knew I was. The old man wasn't just charming. He was crafty as well.

"Kathleen, what do you know about dowsing?" he asked.

I was surprised by the sudden change in the conversation. "Not a lot," I said. "I know it's been used to find groundwater among other things. The practice dates back centuries. Traditionally the dowser uses a forked branch from a tree or a bush—quite often willow or witch hazel—although some prefer using two metal rods. And dowsing is no more effective than just random chance."

He nodded. "I know it shouldn't work. I know there's no science, but there are some things in life that science just can't explain."

I thought about Owen and Hercules and their skills.

"I've seen a dowser find water when no one else could. It's like they have some kind of sixth sense or instinct that comes into play, and you have the same thing when it comes to getting to the truth. Just rely on your instincts and everything will be just fine."

I stayed for another half an hour and we talked about the increase in tourists the town had seen this summer. Harrison told me more about the original Last Bash and how he hoped this revival wouldn't be just a onetime thing.

I finally got to my feet. Boris was in between our chairs and I reached down to scratch his head.

"Stay where you are," I said, leaning down to give Harrison a hug. "I should have a couple of books for you by the end of the week. I'll call you and one of the boys can pick them up."

"Thank you, my dear," he said. "You always do the right thing by me."

I knew he was referring to Mike's death but I let the comment go.

I went out the porch door and walked around the side of the house. As I headed toward the truck, Harry came out of his house and started toward me. I wondered if he'd been watching for me.

"You're heading out," he said when we met by the back bumper of the truck.

"I am," I said. "Thanks again for supper."

He let out a breath. "Kathleen, I'm not going to dance all around the farm. You know Mike and I go way back."

I nodded.

"I haven't known you nearly as long, but I consider you a friend as well. And without you, well, who knows if we would ever have found Elizabeth."

"I feel the same way about you, about all of you," I said.

He shifted uncomfortably from one foot to the other. "I'm sorry to presume on that friendship, but I need you to look into what happened to Mike. I'm not trying to say that Marcus isn't good at his job, but people talk to you because you're not the police. You can find out things Marcus can't."

I wanted to remind him of all the reasons it wasn't a good idea. Instead all I said was "No promises."

He nodded. "That's more than enough."

We said good night and I got in the truck. I hadn't made any promises or actually agreed to anything. Harry might have said that was more than enough, but I wasn't so sure it was.

chapter 6

I had a restless night. I woke up before my alarm went off, even before Owen had the chance to poke me with a paw. I got to the library early and spent a couple of minutes walking around outside, checking the gazebo at the back—no hay bales or swimming pools—and the vegetables and flowers that the summer camp kids were growing in Harry's raised beds. Harry had already begun clearing a space next to the far end of the building for the cold frames. It was just another example of how kind and conscientious he was. I'd meant every word I'd said to him: I did think of him as a friend. Even though I wasn't sure what I could uncover about Mike's death, I knew I had to try.

I spent some time on my laptop at lunchtime but I didn't learn much more about Mike. He had been the top-rated endodontist in the state on Rate My Dentist. I didn't see how his killer could have been a disgruntled patient.

It was a quiet day, maybe because it wasn't raining, and I got the chance to work on my presentation for the library board about the new library computers. They had approved the idea in theory. Now that we had started fund-raising it was time for more details.

As I drove up the hill at the end of the day, I decided I would go talk to Rebecca to see what she could tell me about Mike Bishop and his family. She had grown up in Mayville Heights and she often knew where the bodies were buried, so to speak.

Before I had supper, I pulled some radishes from my little backyard garden and gathered a few more sungold tomatoes to take over to Rebecca after I'd eaten. Hercules sat at one corner of the raised bed watching me—and keeping his feet dry—while Owen walked around the edge, lifting one paw a couple of times as if telling me which tomatoes to pick. I wasn't really sure what I was hoping to learn from Rebecca. Mike's life seemed like an open book. Most of us had at least one person in our lives who wasn't really a fan, but no one had a bad word to say about Mike. He didn't seem like the kind of person to have any skeletons in his closet, but if they were there, Rebecca would probably know about them.

"I'm not sure there's anything I can do to figure this out,"

I said to the boys as I chopped three of the tomatoes for my own supper. "Harry said people tell me things, things that they don't tell Marcus, but I'm not sure it matters this time."

"Mrr," Hercules said.

I wasn't sure if he was agreeing, disagreeing or wondering when we were going to eat.

Marcus had said very little about the investigation but I didn't think he had any suspects at this point. "What if Mike was just the victim of a random crime? What if someone broke in intending to steal whatever they could find and things just went wrong?"

Hercules seemed to consider the idea for a moment.

"Harrison and Harry think I can do something, but maybe I can't. I know that most victims of violent crime know their attacker, but sometimes things are just random."

I was talking out loud mainly just to work things out for myself. I didn't expect either cat to offer any theories on Mike Bishop's death, so I wasn't surprised to look over my shoulder and see that Owen didn't seem to be paying attention at all. He was peering under the refrigerator at something.

"What are you doing?" I said.

One ear twitched but that was the only indication I got that he was listening. He swiped one paw under the fridge and sent a small refrigerator magnet skittering across the floor to stop by my feet. I bent down to pick it up.

It was one that Maggie had given to me. I hadn't been able to find it for a while and I had suspected it might have ended up in the stash of things Owen kept hidden—more or less—in the basement. Owen loved Maggie and had swiped her scarf and one of her mittens among other things in the past.

The magnet was a photo of Einstein with the quote: "God does not play dice with the universe." In other words there is a pattern to things, a plan. Owen cocked his head to one side and looked at me with an almost smug look on his furry face.

"'Not only does God play dice but he sometimes confuses us by throwing them where they cannot be seen,'" I said. "Stephen Hawking."

I raised one eyebrow at Owen in my best Mr. Spock–from–*Star Trek* fashion and returned his smug expression. Then two things occurred to me. One, I was being smug over besting a cat. And two, both Einstein and Hawking were talking about quantum mechanics, not murder.

After supper I walked across the backyard to Rebecca's. I found her cutting lettuce from her own small garden with a tiny pair of kitchen shears. She smiled when she caught sight of me. "Kathleen, your timing is perfect," she said. "The lettuce is taking over. Please tell me you'll take some."

"I'll definitely take some. Mine hasn't grown nearly as well as yours." I held up the brown paper bag I was carrying. "I brought tomatoes and radishes."

"Splendid," Rebecca said. "Everett will eat tomatoes at every meal and I have very few radishes. I think the racoons are having them for a midnight snack."

I watched as she finished filling her colander with lettuce. Then she gestured at the gazebo. "Do you have time to sit in the shade for a bit?" she asked.

"I do," I said.

Rebecca put the lettuce on the small table in the middle of the space and we each took a chair. She folded her hands in her lap. She was tiny with bright blue eyes and silver-gray hair cropped into a short cut that showed off her cheekbones and long neck.

"Where would you like me to start?" she asked. "You are looking for information about Michael's family, aren't you?"

There was no point in pretending I didn't understand what she was referring to. "How did you know?" I asked.

"You and Harrison are very close. I knew he'd ask you to see what you could find out about Michael's death." She frowned. "I'm not wrong, am I?"

I shook my head. "No, you're not."

"So tell me, what would you like to know?"

"The thing is, I'm not really sure," I said. "Did Mike have any enemies? Was there anyone who would have had any reason to want him dead?"

"Your Marcus asked me the same questions," Rebecca said, "and the answers are no and no. Michael was a good man. He was generous with his time, with his skills and with his money."

"Some of that was Finnamore family money?"

Rebecca nodded. "The Finnamore family started Black Dog Boots more than a hundred years ago and they also made money in the timber industry. And before you think either of those businesses could be the cause of Michael's death, you should know that the Finnamores only own a tiny share of either business now. Michael's mother, Elizabeth Finnamore Bishop, inherited her father's share of both companies and, as an only child, all of his money. There's also a separate trust that provides for Finnamore descendants—it pays for college. Elizabeth started a charitable foundation with the money she inherited. It supports several educational organizations—education was one of Elizabeth's favorite causes—as well as a number of school food programs all over the state. I know that Michael continued his mother's work and expanded the school food project. He also started a project to provide basic dental care to children who wouldn't otherwise get it. I don't think anyone is going to commit murder over feeding hungry children or fixing their teeth."

Neither did I.

She nudged her glasses up her nose. "I'm guessing all of that will go to Lachlan now."

"Not Eloise or Jonas?" I asked.

"Eloise lives in California. I don't see how she could run the foundation from out there."

"And Jonas isn't a biological Finnamore."

"Yes." She picked a dried rose petal off the front of her

shirt. "Jonas is probably the trustee for now, but the Finnamore money always stays in the family." She made a face when she said the word "family." "The older generation—Leitha's generation—cared way too much about the bloodline as far as I'm concerned."

"What about Mike?" I asked. "He was digging into the family tree. Do you think he cared about the bloodline?"

"Goodness no!" Rebecca said, gesturing with one hand. "I once heard him tell Leitha it was all a bunch of foolishness. He said the sainted Finnamores weren't any better than anyone else."

"What about Jonas?" I asked. "Do you think his not being a Finnamore matters to him?"

"I'm not sure. I think in some ways he might be relieved not to be. He inherited some land from his father and some invest-ments from Mary-Margaret and he's done well for himself. He's smart and hardworking. Leitha used that family money like a whip to get people to do what she wanted them to. She couldn't do that with Jonas and he was always pretty good at keeping Lachlan out of that." She smiled. "I can see both of their mothers' influence in Michael and in Jonas."

"You knew both women." I pulled one foot up under-neath me.

"I knew Mary-Margaret better," Rebecca said. "I used to cut her hair and she adored both of her boys, Jonas and Colin, Lachlan's father. When Jonas had mumps as a teenager and ran a very high fever, Mary-Margaret wouldn't leave his side at the hospital and Elizabeth had a doctor removed from treating the boy when the doctor tried to send Mary-Margaret home because Jonas wasn't her 'real' son."

"I think I would have liked both of them."

Rebecca smiled again. "You would have. Mary-Margaret was the quieter of the two. Michael is . . . was very much like his mother."

I tried to picture the rough family tree Mike had sketched out as he found new family members. I wasn't sure if any of his family history had anything to do with his murder but it was a place to start, something to at least eliminate. "So Leitha was Elizabeth and Mary-Margaret's aunt," I said.

Rebecca nodded. "That's right. Leitha and John were brother and sister." She tapped one finger on the table as though she was plotting out the family connections. "Leitha had one child, Eloise. Her brother, John, had two daughters, Elizabeth and Mary-Margaret, which made Leitha great-aunt to Michael—and Jonas as far as I'm concerned. Did you meet Eloise when she was here for her mother's service?"

"I did," I said. "She came into the library to see all the work that had been done."

"She was estranged from her mother, you know."

I shook my head. "I didn't know that, but I'm not really surprised. Leitha had a strong personality." And equally strong opinions I'd learned the first time we'd met. She told me with no beating around the bush that she believed the money spent on renovating the library had been nothing more than "foolish sentimentality." She thought the building should have been torn down and replaced with a new, modern structure.

The Mayville Heights Free Public Library was a Carnegie library and much of the town's history was tied up with it. Not to mention it was an excellent example of the architecture of its time. All of which I had nicely explained to Leitha. None of which had changed her mind.

"The woman had some very old-fashioned ideas," Rebecca said, pursing her lips with disapproval. "Eloise has two daughters. They're both adopted."

"You think that estrangement had something to do with them not being biological Finnamores?"

Rebecca sighed. "I hope not, but knowing Leitha, it wasn't impossible. She was missing out on so much not being in those girls' lives. Look how blessed I am by having Ami."

Ami was Everett's granddaughter. Rebecca had been part of her life since she was a little girl. Even when Everett and Rebecca weren't part of each other's lives, she and Ami had stayed close.

"There's no blood tie between us, but I couldn't love Ami any more if there was. What binds people is love, not strands of DNA." She reached out one hand and gently waved a butterfly away from the lettuce. "You know, some people think the Finnamores are cursed."

I shifted in my chair. The foot I'd been sitting on was going to sleep. "Do you?"

Rebecca shook her head. "No. I don't believe in silly things like that. The rain falls equally on sinner and saint and there were both in that family, just like in any other family, no matter what Leitha would have liked the rest of us to believe."

"Do you know how the family came to start Black Dog Boots?" I asked. I had found very little about the history of the company when I'd been prowling around on their website at lunchtime.

"Leitha's grandfather started Black Dog. He started out as a lumberjack, but he saved every penny and eventually had his own crew of men. Black Dog began because he couldn't find durable work boots. Except for a minor share, the business was sold years ago, so if you're thinking Michael was killed by a disgruntled employee"—she held up both hands—"I think you're looking in the wrong direction."

"Do you think there could be any connection between Mike's death and the band?" I felt like I was just pulling random ideas out of the air now.

"I don't see how," Rebecca said. "Everyone was thrilled that they had gotten together again. In fact, I wouldn't have been surprised to see them do more shows together. No one thought that was a bad idea, but Harry or Johnny could tell you more about that."

I couldn't think of anything else to ask her, especially since I had already taken more of her time than I'd intended. We talked about our respective vegetable patches for a moment and then I thanked Rebecca for the lettuce and the information and headed home.

Owen had moved from walking around the vegetable bed to sitting on the arm of one of the Adirondack chairs. I joined him. He sniffed the lettuce out of curiosity but made a face. Salad didn't interest him, other than the croutons if there were any, although he had been known to lick the ranch dressing off a bit of cucumber that accidentally landed on the floor.

The cat glanced over toward Rebecca's yard and then gave me a curious look.

"Nothing useful," I said, assuming he wanted to know what I'd learned from Rebecca when maybe he was just wondering if she had any yellow catnip chickens. "I did learn that Mike's great-grandfather was a lumberjack but I don't see how that's going to help me."

Marcus came around the side of the house then. He was carrying one of Burtis's potato baskets.

"Hi," I said.

"Hi, yourself," he said. He held up the basket. "New potatoes for you from Burtis via Brady."

I smiled. Burtis grew some of the best potatoes I'd ever eaten. "Please thank both of them and thank *you* for bringing them over."

"You're very welcome," Marcus said. He leaned down to kiss me, set the basket on the grass and lowered himself into the other chair.

Owen jumped down from his perch on the arm of my chair and walked over to peer at the potatoes. Before I could stop him, he jumped into the basket.

"Get out of there," I said.

He looked at me, not even blinking.

"Get out," I repeated.

His response was to disappear.

I blew out a breath in frustration, lifting my bangs off my face. "I know you're there, Owen," I said.

Marcus laughed.

"Don't laugh," I said. "It just encourages him."

"Did you know that researchers in Montreal have been looking at ways to change a light's frequency to make it pass through an object, which then makes the object seem to be invisible?"

We could both see a potato moving in the basket.

"Clearly those researchers weren't working with any cats," I said.

Marcus stretched out his long legs and raked a hand through his hair. He was frustrated.

"The Bishop case?" I asked.

He nodded. "I have no suspects and almost no evidence. Mike Bishop died of a head injury, but no one in the area heard or saw anything and the man was universally well-liked."

"According to Rebecca, some people think the Finnamore family is cursed." The potato was still moving, pushed I knew by a furry gray-and-white paw.

"You think Rebecca really believes that?" Marcus asked.

I pulled both feet up onto the seat of my chair and wrapped my arms around my legs. "No. And for the record, neither do

I. As Rebecca put it, 'The rain falls equally on sinner and saint and there were both in that family.' The quote comes from the Bible, in case you were wondering."

"I don't believe in things like jinxes or curses," he said.

I gave a snort of laughter. "This from the man who wouldn't wash his hockey jersey during the playoffs last year."

He was already shaking his head. "That's different. When I don't wash my jersey, I'm connecting with the collective mindset of hockey fans all over the country. Our shared energy supports the team."

"More like a shared delusion, but who am I to argue?" I said. I rested my chin on one knee.

"Something else I don't believe in?" Marcus said. "Coincidences. The deaths of two people in the same family in just three months doesn't feel right to me."

"It happens," I said.

I'd always felt a little sad about Leitha Anderson's death. She had come to the library for a talk about the history of the area given by Mary. Previous lectures in the series had included two talks by Harrison and one by Everett. Mary and Leitha had had a very loud and very public argument after Mary's talk. On the drive home, Leitha had suffered a heart attack, gone off the road and died before paramedics arrived.

"Mike was murdered. Leitha was old and her death was an accident," I said.

Marcus looked away for a moment; then his eyes met mine again. "What if it wasn't?"

chapter 7

I had no words. I just stared at him. "Are you serious?" I finally managed to say. "You really think there's a connection between Mike's death and his great-aunt's? Leitha died in a car accident. Mike was murdered. I don't see it."

"I'm not saying there is a connection," Marcus said. "Right now all I'm doing is speculating, but I do know there is a lot of money in the Finnamore family trust."

"'If money go before, all ways do lie open,'" I said softly. "Shakespeare."

I nodded. *The Merry Wives of Windsor.* I lifted my chin from my knee and stretched out my legs again. "So who benefited from their deaths?" It was a question Marcus often considered in a murder case.

"As far as I can see, Jonas and Lachlan Quinn."

"You can eliminate Jonas, because he isn't a biological Finnamore, so he didn't benefit from either Mike's or Leitha's deaths because he can't inherit anything involving the trust. And as for Lachlan, he's seventeen. C'mon, you can't really believe a teenager engineered Leitha's death to look like an accident and did such a good job that up to now no one suspected anything and *then* on top of that he managed to kill Mike. Lachlan seems like a bright kid but I remember myself at that age and I wasn't smart enough to pull that off. Were you?"

Marcus leaned over and kissed the side of my face. "I couldn't figure out how to get girls to notice me when I was seventeen. I wouldn't have been capable of plotting to kill anyone." He laughed; then his expression became serious again. "Just between the two of us, hypothetically, what do you think happened?"

"Hypothetically, I keep coming back to the idea of some random thief who was surprised by Mike and panicked."

"But?" He raised an eyebrow. "There is a but, isn't there?"

I leaned my head against the back of the chair. "Again, hypothetically speaking, if the police, if you, had any evidence that led in that direction—any sign of a break-in, missing valuables, someone suspicious seen around Mike's house or if there had been other break-ins in the neighborhood—you wouldn't be looking for a connection to Leitha's death."

He didn't say anything, which in itself told me I was right.

Hercules came across the lawn from the direction of Rebecca's yard. He eyed the basket of potatoes and then jumped onto my lap, nuzzling my chin before murping a hello to Marcus.

"This isn't going to be easy," I said as much to myself as to Marcus or the cat.

"No," Marcus agreed, "it isn't."

Harry arrived at the library about midmorning on Tuesday. I was reshelving some reference books and spotted him out the window. I set the last book on the shelf and walked over to the circulation desk. "I'm just going outside to talk to Harry for a minute," I said to Susan, who was working the desk.

She was sorting through a stack of children's picture books, pulling an odd assortment of things that seemed to have been used as bookmarks from between the pages. There were a folded sticky note, a scrap of red yarn, a swizzle stick and three squares of toilet paper piled next to her right arm. She looked up at me, nudging her cat's-eye glasses up her nose with one knuckle. "Take your time." She dipped her head at the heap of would-be bookmarks. "People use the oddest things to mark their place."

"Yes, they do," I agreed, struggling to keep a straight face since Susan herself was anchoring her topknot with a bamboo knife and fork.

I walked across the parking lot and Harry got to his feet when he saw me approaching, brushing the dirt off his hands.

"Good morning," he said. "The old man told me next time I saw you to be sure to tell you that those tomatoes are the best so far."

"I'm glad he liked them. I'll get some more out to him. I have more than I can use." I looked over the flower bed. "The marigolds still look good."

"They should be fine until the first frost." He adjusted the brim of his ball cap. "You didn't come out here to talk about tomatoes and flowers, Kathleen."

"No, I didn't," I said. "I need you to tell me about Mike. The real person. Don't get me wrong. I liked him. But I know that people tend to make a person into a saint when they're dead."

Harry smiled. "Mike definitely wasn't a saint, but he was a good guy. In all the years I've known"—he stopped, took a breath and let it out and then continued—"knew Mike, I think I may have seen him lose his temper five or six times if that. He was just one of those people who could roll with whatever was happening. That was the real Mike."

"How did you all manage to practice for the show without the people around you finding out?"

"I think a few people did guess, but they were just good at keeping the secret," Harry said. "I'm pretty sure the old man figured it out, although he says he didn't. Mike came over to the house every Thursday night for weeks so we could practice together because it was the only time we could make it work. Monday through Wednesday he worked later at the office and Friday night he was checking out new music somewhere in the area. Peggy works late on Thursdays, so dad was always around and you know he doesn't miss a thing."

I smiled. "No, he doesn't." I also knew Harrison was very good at keeping his own counsel, to use one of his own expressions.

"Eventually, we worked things out so the others could join in on Zoom. Mike set everything up. I did ask Larry a couple of computer questions, but I don't think he figured it out." He shrugged. "Then again, for all I know, maybe I'm selling him short. I can tell you that Mike was never late, so I'm guessing someone in his office knew he was doing something even if they didn't know what the something was, because they got him out on time every single Thursday. And we all spent a couple of Saturdays at Paul's camp. It's likely Paul's wife, Sonja, knew or guessed what was going on."

He frowned. "Do you think someone had been watching Mike's coming and goings and broke into the house when they thought he wouldn't show up?"

I played with my watch, twisting it around my arm. I wasn't sure about anything. "I don't know," I said. "Right now anything is possible."

Later that morning Johnny Rock came in to the library. I was standing in the doorway to our smaller meeting room talking to Patricia Queen, head of the quilters group that met each week in the library, when Susan came to find me. Patricia and I were talking about a fall workshop for beginning quilters. We'd already had one quilt show at the library, which had shown me there was lots of interest in the craft.

"Kathleen, I'm sorry for interrupting," Susan said. "Johnny Rock is here to see you and he says it's important."

"That's all right," Patricia said before I had a chance to speak. "We covered everything I had on my list and I'll e-mail you the notes on our meeting this afternoon." Patricia was nothing if not organized.

"Thank you," I said. "If anything else comes to mind after I've read your notes, I'll be in touch."

Patricia picked up her quilted tote bag, tucked the small notepad and pen she'd been using inside, nodded to both of us and strode purposefully though the stacks.

Susan and I followed behind her, a little less briskly.

"Kathleen, do you think Patricia would come to my house and teach the boys some organization skills?" Susan asked.

Her boys, twins, were incredibly smart, genius-level-IQ smart. They were always coming up with some new project, which always seemed to take the entire house to put together.

"You know, she probably would," I said.

Susan made a face. "Doing that seems kind of mean," she said, "to Patricia."

"You know, if the three of them teamed up, between the boys' creative thinking and Patricia's organizing skills, they could take over the world."

She grimaced. "Did I say getting the three of them together would be mean? Make that scary. Very scary."

Johnny was waiting for me by the circulation desk. He gestured to the carved wooden sun over the front entrance with the words *Let there be light*. "You know, I'm a bit embarrassed to admit I never noticed those words before," he said.

"You're not the only one, I promise. The same words are over the entrance to the very first Carnegie library in Dunfermline in Scotland."

Johnny looked around the large open space. "I'm glad the building was restored," he said. "It would be a shame to lose such a big part of the town's history."

"I agree," I said.

He turned his attention back to me. "Kathleen, could we talk somewhere a little more private?"

"Of course." I gestured toward the stairs to the second floor. "Come up to my office."

I led the way up and unlocked my office door. "How about a cup of coffee?" I asked.

"Yes, please," he said. "Black with one sugar would be great."

"Have a seat." I indicated the two chairs in front of my desk. "I'll be right back."

I went down to the staff room, got coffee for the two of us and went back to my office.

"What did you need to talk to me about?" I asked after I'd set our mugs on my desk. Instead of sitting across the desk from Johnny, I had taken the other chair next to him.

"You brought the library back to life," he said. "And I don't just mean with the restoration of the actual building. You've made the library a big part of the community, the way it used to be. The way it should be."

I took a sip of my coffee before I answered. "Thank you," I said. "It took a lot of work from a lot of people to make it all happen. I can't take all the credit. I shouldn't."

"Mike talked a lot about how much help you gave him while he worked on his family history."

I smiled. "He was so caught up in learning more about the family, it was easy to get carried along with his enthusiasm. I enjoyed myself. He brought coffee and muffins for my staff twice. We all liked him."

Johnny handed me an envelope.

"What is this?" I asked.

"Mike wasn't one for showy remembrances, but I wanted . . . I *need* to do something in his memory." He cleared his throat. "Harry said the library is fund-raising for new computers." He indicated the envelope. "I hope that will help."

I lifted the flap and was stunned to see the amount of the

check inside. It would take us past our fund-raising goal. I pressed my lips together and swallowed down the sudden press of tears. "Thank you. This is so incredibly generous. I promise to make sure everyone knows the new computers are in memory of Mike."

Johnny smiled. "Thank you. I think Mike would get a kick out of that. I'll let the guys know and Mike's family as well." He got to his feet and I did the same, still holding tightly to that check. "You know, it's going to be odd on Thursday nights not to be getting together with the guys online to make music. Those few hours feel as though they've left a gaping hole in my life."

"You gave everyone who was at the concert something we're going to remember for the rest of our lives," I said.

I walked Johnny back downstairs, thanked him again and then stood in the entrance and watched him cross the parking lot to talk to Harry. I went back inside to find Susan stacking books on a cart. She looked up at me.

"Johnny made a donation in memory of Mike, didn't he?" she said

I nodded. "Enough to put our new-computer fund over the top."

She grinned and did a little fist pump. "Do you remember that Saturday Mike was here and he fixed the computer monitor for that kid who was working on a paper for school? Last minute, of course."

I nodded. Mike had tried so hard not to swear because there

were kids around. After the monitor was working again, he'd told me our computers were a bunch of boat anchors with a few colorful adjectives added. I pictured him standing by the circulation desk, just about where Susan was standing now, hands gesturing in the air.

"You're going to figure out who did this, right?" Susan asked.

"That's Marcus's job," I said.

Susan nudged her glasses up her nose and brushed a stray strand of hair off her face. "I know," she said. "And you're going to figure out who did this, right?"

I could still see Mike, in my mind, standing there telling me that the library needed to have computers from this century. I nodded. "Right," I said.

chapter 8

I got home to find Hercules on the back step with a grackle feather under one paw and a triumphant look on his face.

"Don't tell me that you two are at it again?" I said.

He looked down at the feather and then looked at me. "Merow," he said.

The cat and one particular grackle—or maybe it was several different birds for all I knew—had had some kind of war going on for quite some time. Basically neither wanted to share the backyard with the other. They had seemed to reach a détente earlier in the summer, but now it seemed the battle was on again.

I had always had the feeling that the two of them liked their little skirmishes. If one took down the other, the fun would be over. I'd seen the grackle sweep low, just inches over the cat's head, several different times. To me, it looked liked the same bird. I'd discovered that the average life span of a grackle was about seventeen years, so it wasn't that unlikely that Hercules had been warring with the same bird from the beginning. This wasn't the first time he had snagged one of the bird's feathers. Last week the grackle had swiped two sardine crackers from the arm of one of the Adirondack chairs, just inches from Herc's nose. Was this some kind of retaliation or had Hercules found the feather on the lawn and brought it home as a trophy

I unlocked the porch door. "Leave that out here," I said, indicating the feather.

He wrinkled his nose at me.

"The spoils of battle stay outside," I said firmly.

He looked at the feather, sighed and came inside.

I changed for tai chi class and warmed up a bowl of noodles and veggies for supper. Hercules sulked around the kitchen. I found the little mechanical mouse Marcus had brought back for him after a recent trip. He'd gotten Owen a catnip frog, Ferdinand the Funky Frog, to be precise, sibling, via adoption, to Owen's beloved Fred the Funky Chicken. Since Hercules didn't get the attraction of catnip his gift was the mouse.

I set the mouse going and put it on the floor. Hercules liked to watch it run randomly all over the kitchen and then whack it with a paw. Once he'd smacked the little toy so hard, it skidded across the floor all the way to the living room doorway.

Owen wandered in for a drink, and when the tiny mouse suddenly veered in his direction, bushing against the end of his tail, he started with a loud meow. His paw hit the edge of the dish and flipped it into the air like someone doing a trick with a Frisbee. I sucked in a breath, picturing water everywhere and a wet, indignant cat, but luckily the bowl was empty and it landed right side up on the floor.

"You're fine," I said. "No water. No harm done."

I spoke too soon.

The mouse was still moving, veering to the right, toward Hercules, who slapped a paw on it and looked at us with triumph in his green eyes.

Owen glared at his brother, taking a step back and unfortunately putting his foot in Herc's water dish. Owen let out a yowl of annoyance, vigorously shaking his back right foot. Hercules made an equally annoyed grumble because he very much did not like Owen putting even a whisker near his dishes. Somehow the mouse got out from under Hercules's foot, spun around in a circle and headed for the back door as though trying to get away from what was shaping up to be a monumental cat argument.

I walked around the table and pointed a finger at Hercules, who was already starting for his brother. "Not another step, mister," I said.

"Merow!" he replied with a fair amount of indignation, pleading his case as it were.

"It was an accident. They happen." They seemed to happen a lot in this house but that wasn't the point.

Owen gave me his best I-have-been-injured look and shook his foot. I bent down and picked him up, using the hem of my shirt to wipe his foot. It was only a little damp. I stroked the top of his head.

"It was just an accident," I repeated. "It's not your brother's fault."

He continued to mutter almost under his breath.

I set Owen down next to the basement door. I looked from one cat to the other. "Don't move."

Owen's front left paw twitched.

"Don't push it," I warned.

The paw stopped moving and Owen contented himself with making a show of *not* looking in his brother's direction, while Hercules darted sideways looks at his sibling.

I gave each cat a cracker. "I'm probably weakening your character by doing this," I told them. That didn't seem to be a concern for either one of them.

I wiped up the tiny bit of water on the floor and rinsed all four bowls. Roma had suggested a fountain for the cats. Maybe it was something I should consider.

I retrieved the mouse from the back door and put it in the cupboard with the cat treats. I realized I just had time to change my T-shirt before tai chi if I wanted to walk down to class.

Owen had eaten his cracker and he followed me upstairs, immediately going to sit in front of the closet door. I thought of him as the feline fashion police. I held up a T-shirt and he wrinkled his whiskers. He didn't like my second choice, either, but he seemed happy with my third pick. I pulled my hair into a ponytail and went back downstairs.

I didn't have time to do my own dishes, so I stacked them in the sink and grabbed my bag with my towel and tai chi shoes. Hercules was in the porch looking out the window.

"Please give Owen some space," I said.

"Mrr," he said.

I hoped that was acquiescence.

It was the perfect night for walking, warm but not overwhelmingly hot. When I got to the studio, I discovered that the stairwell and the area where we hung up our things and changed our shoes had gotten a fresh coat of paint. The clean, bright white walls made the space seem a little larger.

Maggie was inside, standing by the window with a mug of tea. I walked over to join her.

"The entry looks great," I said.

She smiled. "I can't believe what a difference just a coat of paint makes. I didn't realize how dingy the walls looked until the painters started working."

"Who did the work? I know you couldn't have used Oren because he's out of town." Oren Kenyon was a very talented carpenter and a meticulous painter. He was away for a few days supervising the installation of several pieces of his father's artwork in a gallery in Madison.

"It's a company run by a bunch of students just for the summer," Maggie said. "And it was actually Oren who suggested them, so that was enough of a recommendation for me. *And* you'll never guess who one of the painters turned out to be? Zach Redmond."

Zach had been bartending at The Brick, a club up on the highway. He was one of Maggie's yoga students and I'd met him when my brother and his band had visited and we'd gone to the club to listen to a group Ethan had wanted to check out. Zach wore his thick dark hair in a man bun most of the time. He had dark skin and beautiful blue eyes.

"I thought he'd gone back to school," I said.

She took a sip of her tea. It smelled like marmalade. "He's still working on his degree and he's doing some shifts at The Brick and painting during the day."

Zach was still trying to figure out what he wanted to do with his life. I remembered how Maggie had described him to me: "He's like a big untrained puppy. Sometimes you have to smack him on the nose with a rolled-up newspaper."

Maggie smiled. "You know how Zach has always lacked, well, focus?"

I nodded.

"I overheard him talking to the young woman he was working with, warning her about drinking too much, staying out late and borrowing stuff from her grandmother without asking."

"Sound like he's maturing," I said.

Roma joined us then. Her dark hair was pulled back in a stubby ponytail and she was wearing a sea green sleeveless T-shirt and cropped gray leggings. "We match," she said, holding out the hem of her shirt. My top was just a slightly darker version of the shade of green she was wearing.

"Truthfully, Owen picked it out," I said.

"Hey, you have a fashion consultant. That's great," she said, grinning and bumping me with her shoulder. "I was going through photos Eddie took at the concert and there are some good ones of you and Marcus. First chance I get this week, I'll send them and some of the others to you."

"Thank you," I said. "I didn't think about taking pictures and now I wish I had."

"You're welcome. Eddie loves any chance to use that fancy camera. Ruby has been giving him some tips."

Ruby Blackthorne, a very talented artist and photographer, was a member of the local artists' co-op.

"I need to go speak to Rebecca," Roma said. "Eddie got a beautiful shot of her and Everett dancing."

As though saying her name had suddenly conjured her out of thin air, Ruby appeared in the doorway. She crossed the room and joined us.

"I have something to show you," she said, a huge smile lighting up her face.

"Is it the new calendar?" I asked.

Ruby had taken some photos of Owen and Hercules, and that had morphed into a very successful promotional calendar for the town. So successful that now there was a second one, once again featuring the boys at various locations around town.

Ruby nodded and held out the large envelope she was holding. "Take a look."

The calendar's cover photo was Owen and Hercules on the deck of a sailboat. I remembered that shoot. Owen had shown no trepidation about getting on the boat but Hercules had been very reluctant. Given his intense dislike of wet feet, that hadn't surprised me. Ruby had shamelessly bribed him with a dish of chopped roast beef.

Maggie and I flipped through the calendar pages. "Oh, I like this one!" I exclaimed about the photo that had been taken of the boys in the same spot we were standing. Owen was on his back legs with his front paws on the window ledge. Hercules was sitting on the ledge, one paw in the air almost as though he was working on his tai chi form.

"Look, Owen's doing Cloud Hands," Maggie teased. "He's good, too." Cloud Hands was one of the 108 movements of the form that still gave me grief.

I stuck my tongue out at her and she laughed. Then she bent her head over the calendar again.

"I like the lighting in this one," she said to Ruby. "You've done an incredible job."

I nodded my agreement. "I didn't think it was possible, but this one is even better than the first calendar."

Ruby's cheeks flushed at the compliments. "You can keep that one and take it home for Owen and Hercules to see."

"Thank you," I said, slipping the calendar back inside the envelope.

"I'm going to get a cup of tea," Ruby said. "I'm glad you like the calendar."

Maggie took another sip of her own tea while stretching one arm over her head. "How was your day?" she asked. Maggie was the kind of person who was genuinely interested when she asked a question like that.

"Johnny Rock came in to make a donation in Mike's memory to our computer fund," I said. "It put us over the top."

"I think that's a great memorial for Mike."

"It is. There are a lot of people who depend on us for Internet access and just for the chance to even use a computer. I'm happy that now we have the money to replace all the old ones."

"But you wish it wasn't because Mike's dead." She switched arms, stretching her left one now.

"Exactly," I said. "He called the old ones boat anchors, which isn't far from the truth."

"So he'd be happy you're getting new ones."

I rubbed the back of my neck with one hand. "I think so, yes."

"So you should be happy, too."

"What would I do without you?" I said.

"You'd never master Cloud Hands, you and Marcus would not be a couple and you'd let your cat pick out your clothes all the time," she teased.

I wrapped her in a hug. "Then lucky for me that I came to Mayville Heights."

"Lucky for me, too," Maggie said.

It was almost time to begin. Maggie and I walked over to the tea table.

"Has anyone from Mike Bishop's office called you?" she asked.

I frowned at her. "No. Why would they be calling?"

Maggie ran a hand over her blond curls. "Well, I heard from them because I had an appointment coming up and Caroline wanted to let me know what my options are."

Caroline was Mike Bishop's office manager. She was someone I should talk to, I realized.

"They're going to call every patient at some point to see what people want to do with their records." She set her cup on the table. "Has Marcus has come up with anything yet?"

I sighed softly. "No."

"Have you?"

There wasn't any point in denying that I was asking questions about Mike's death. I shook my head. "No."

"You'll figure it out," Maggie said, giving my arm a squeeze as she moved to the center of the room. She clapped her hands and called, "Circle, everyone."

I darted out to put the calendar in my bag. Then I moved

into my usual spot next to Roma and it struck me that I didn't know if Maggie had been referring to both Marcus and me when she'd said, "You'll figure it out," or if she'd just meant me.

When we finished the form at the end of the class, I was surprised to see Marcus waiting by the door. He walked over to me. "Can I lure you out for frozen yogurt at Tubby's?" he asked. "Or do you need to get home?"

I smiled. "I can always find time for Tubby's," I said.

"Good," he said. He turned to Maggie. "Brady showed me your design ideas for the T-shirts for the girls' hockey team. I don't know how we're going to pick just one."

"It was fun working on them," Maggie said. "And it wasn't just me. Kathleen and Owen both offered their input."

Marcus smiled. "I'll make sure both of them are rewarded."

I changed my shoes and we headed down the stairs.

"Where did you park?" Marcus asked as we stepped outside. "I didn't see the truck anywhere."

"I walked," I said. "It was such a nice evening and I spent a lot of time sitting today. I wanted to stretch my legs."

His SUV was parked just ahead. "That works out perfectly. We can drive over to Tubby's for yogurt and find a place to enjoy it along the Riverwalk. I'll take you home after that."

I recognized his matter-of-fact tone. He was in detective mode.

We got to the car, and before I got inside, I stopped, resting one hand on the roof. "Marcus, I'm always happy to see you and I'm always up for frozen yogurt, but I know you're here for more than that. So please tell me what's up."

He looked at the keys in his hand for a moment; then he looked over the roof of the car at me. "I need you to tell me all about Leitha Anderson's visit to the library on the day she died."

My heart began to thump in my ears. "Did you actually find a connection between her death and Mike's?"

He thought for a moment. "Can we just get in, please?" he said.

We both climbed into the SUV and I turned to face him before I even fastened my seat belt. "What's going on?" I said. "Is Leitha's accident connected to Mike's death?"

He stuck the key in the ignition without saying anything, then looked at me. "At this point I can't be sure, but I have reason to believe Leitha Anderson's death wasn't so accidental after all."

chapter 9

I stared at him, wondering if I'd heard him right. "I don't understand," I said. "Leitha had a heart attack. Her car went off the road. Everyone agreed it was an accident."

Marcus did his hand-hair thing. He looked tired. There was dark stubble on his face and lines pulled at his mouth. "I know, but I couldn't let go of the idea that something was off about her death, so I went back through the file on the accident and I noticed that Leitha had been involved in a study on heart disease and longevity."

I nodded. "I know. Mike told me that Leitha was the only person in two generations of their family to live into her nineties."

"It was a long shot, but I contacted one of the doctors who

is involved in that study and I sent him a copy of the medical examiner's report. He called me back less than an hour later and he told me that he had concerns over the levels of potassium chloride in blood samples taken at Leitha's autopsy. According to the doctor, she had used a salt substitute in the past that contained potassium, but not enough to explain the levels found in her blood in his opinion. And as far as he knew, she hadn't been using that substitute anymore."

"If those levels were too high, they could have caused an irregular heart beat and heart failure."

"Exactly," Marcus said.

He fastened his seat belt and started the SUV and we drove over to Tubby's. I got strawberry frozen yogurt. Marcus chose orange cream. We walked along the Riverwalk and sat down on the second bench we saw with our cups of frozen yogurt.

"Tell me what you're thinking," he said.

"I'm thinking that I've always felt bad about Leitha's death," I said.

"Why?" he asked.

"She came to the library for the presentation about the history of Mayville Heights that Mary was giving."

The talks on the history of this part of the state had turned out to be extremely popular. All of them had been well attended.

"And she and Mary ended up having a very loud and very public argument about the early settlement of the town," Marcus said.

I nodded. "Yes." My chest tightened at the memory of their raised voices, particularly the disdain in Leitha's tone. "I had to step in to put a stop to it."

I remembered how Leitha had given Mary her steely gaze and said, "Breeding will tell."

Mary had met the other woman's stare with an equally undaunted look and said, "Yes, it certainly will."

I licked a bit of frozen yogurt off my thumb. "Some people found Leitha to be too blunt and abrasive and they liked seeing Mary stand up to her. I know Mary was sorry for making a scene. She apologized immediately and she came out to the house that night to apologize again.

I had been surprised to see a somber-looking Mary at my door. "May I come in?" she'd asked.

"Of course," I'd said.

"I know I told you this afternoon how sorry I am for getting into an argument with Leitha and making a scene at the library. It was petty and childish of me," she'd said as she stood in the middle of the porch.

"But understandable. Leitha is a challenging person."

"I want you to know that something like that will never happen again. I give you my word. And I'm sorry that I put you in a difficult situation."

"I appreciate that," I'd said. "I don't understand what happened? What made you so angry?"

Mary had looked at the floor for a moment; then her eyes met mine. "Leitha was going on about the Finnamores being among the first settlers in this area. The fact of the matter is it was Ruby's family—the Blackthornes—not the Finnamores who first settled this area. And Keith King's family and Lita's have been here almost as long. I reminded Leitha of that and that the town was actually built where there had been an earlier indigenous settlement." There was a flush of color in her cheeks. This was obviously something she felt strongly about. "You know about Ruby's indigenous ancestry, I'm guessing."

"I do," I'd said.

"In fact Ruby's family was here a couple of generations before the Finnamores, or anyone else for that matter. Leitha was dismissive as though they weren't important because they didn't come over on the *Mayflower*. So I got my knickers in a knot. I should have known it was a waste of time, trying to talk to that woman." Her cheeks got a little pinker and she stuffed her hands in her pockets. "I was wrong for calling Leitha an old bat."

I'd nodded. "It didn't help."

"And I will apologize to her for that," Mary had said.

"Of course she didn't get the chance," I said to Marcus. "She felt bad that maybe their argument had contributed to Leitha's heart attack, which then led to the accident. Leitha was very angry when she left the library. I think Mary still feels a little guilty."

"I can see why she would," he said. "Do you want some of my frozen yogurt?"

"Maybe just a taste," I said.

He held out the cup and I scooped out a spoonful. The orange cream flavor was tart and rich all at the same time. "Oh, that's good," I said. "I'm getting that next time." I offered my own cup. "Would you like to try mine?"

He smiled. "Kathleen, you ate it all," he said.

I tipped up the container to take a look. It was empty. How had that happened?

"Was Mary's talk like the previous ones?" Marcus asked. "Did you offer tea and coffee again?"

"Yes, we did," I said. "Oh, and there were maple cookies from Eric's."

"Did you see Leitha eat a cookie or drink a cup of tea or coffee?"

"You don't think she was poisoned, do you?"

"I didn't say that," he said. "Did you see her eat or drink anything?"

I tried to picture the aftermath of Mary's talk. People had been milling around, getting tea or coffee, talking. More than one person had commented on the cookies.

"Mary offered a cookie to Leitha," I said.

His blue eyes narrowed. "Offered or gave?"

"Mary would not poison Leitha or anyone else. You know Mary. You have to know that."

"I didn't say she did." He waited.

"Offered," I said firmly. "I remember that she was holding the tray." I set my empty yogurt cup on the bench. "You can't possibly think that Mary killed Leitha—that Mary *planned* to kill Leitha—because it's not like she would have had potassium chloride in the pocket of her sweater."

Marcus held up one hand. "I don't believe Mary killed Leitha. I don't believe she would kill anyone—give them a stern talking-to, yes, or in a worst-case scenario maybe drop-kick them across the room, but I don't see her resorting to murder."

I tapped my spoon against my bottom lip. "When would Leitha have to have ingested the potassium chloride for it to have caused her heart attack?"

"The doctor thinks it would have to have been in her system about an hour before the heart attack that caused her to go off the road."

"So at the library," I said.

"It's possible that Leitha had pills on her and took too many by mistake, but I can't find any reference to any kind of medication in any police reports and she hadn't been prescribed potassium chloride by her doctor."

"I didn't see her take anything."

"But you weren't watching her all the time."

I shook my head. "No. There was a lot going on." I looked out over the water for a moment. "Marcus, do you think it's possible that Leitha committed suicide?" I asked.

Marcus stretched one arm along the top of the bench. "I admit that did occur to me, but it doesn't make sense. She was in good physical health, especially for her age and her mind was sharp. I checked with her doctor *and* the doctor running the study—she had no cognitive issues at all. No one who knew Leitha said anything about her seeming depressed. She had plans made several months ahead. Nothing suggests suicide."

"So what happens now?" I asked.

"The medical examiner is doing more tests and consulting with Dr. Faraday, the doctor in charge of the study."

The breeze lifted my hair and I tucked a stray strand back behind my ear. "What happens if they decide that Leitha was murdered? And how does that all connect to Mike's death? Or does it?"

Marcus shrugged. "That's the part I still don't know."

chapter 10

I reached over and laid my hand on Marcus's arm. His skin was warm under my fingers "So what do you do until you get some answers?" I asked.

"I keep working on the Bishop case. Do you remember? Was Mike at the library for Mary's talk?"

"He was. It was a Friday afternoon and his office was closed, so Mike was there."

Marcus linked his fingers with mine. "Do you know if he had started digging into his ancestry at that point?"

I shook my head. "I don't think so. He told me that Leitha's death was actually what inspired him to learn more abut the family, but he seemed very interested in what Mary had to say.

I know he talked to her a couple of times about his great-grandfather when he was working on the family tree."

"Do you remember if Mike came to any of the other lectures?" Marcus asked.

"He was at the second one Harrison gave, and I did see them talking afterward, but they knew each other well, so it didn't mean they were talking about Mike's family tree. Why are you asking? Do you think something Mike uncovered in his family's past has something to do with his death?"

He shrugged. "Right now I'm not ruling anything out. Do you remember when he first came into the library to start researching his family history?"

I straightened the neck of my T-shirt, running my fingers over the stitching around the neck, as I searched my memory for the first time Mike had asked for my help. "I think it was roughly about a month after Leitha's death. He showed up one Friday morning right after we opened.

"Mike said he'd been poking around online on one of those ancestry sites, but he wasn't finding a lot of what he was looking for, and he wanted to know what to do next.

"I made some suggestions—there were some old documents that had been digitized but weren't accessible through the library's website yet and we had some other papers he could look at if he took the proper care, plus old microfilm he could go through. Mike asked if there was a way to borrow certain other documents."

"Do you remember which documents?" Marcus asked.

"A diary, some passenger manifests and some photos. Pretty much all the things he asked about were too fragile to be in circulation, so I told him if he could let me know specifically what he wanted, I should be able to get copies or images of most things for him. And I know he went to Minneapolis to do some research at least once."

Marcus looked thoughtful and I knew he was filing away everything I said, already looking for connections between what he knew and what he was learning.

"Do you remember me telling you about an old map they used on the *Great Northern Baking Showdown*?" I asked.

Eugenie had been very good about working local references into the show whenever she had the chance. When she and Russell had filmed a segment at Wild Rose Bluff, they had used a map from the library in their intro.

Marcus frowned. "It was a map of the area around Wild Rose Bluff?"

I nodded, pushing my hair back off my face again. "Mike looked at that and he was very interested when I told him about an even earlier map showing land claims in the area that had just recently been donated to the library in Red Wing. The librarian there made a copy of it for me."

"Can you think of anything else?"

I shook my head.

"Okay, let's go back to Mary's presentation for a minute. Did Mike sit with Leitha?"

I thought for a moment, trying to picture the meeting

room. "Yes," I said. "Leitha was on the end of a row, Mike was beside her and Jonas Quinn was next to him." I motioned with one hand, slotting people in their seats in my mind. "Harrison was in the row in front of them. And Keith King. Keith has been tracing his family tree ever since Ella got him one of those DNA test kits. And I remember seeing Keith and Mike talking before Mary got started."

Marcus nodded and I knew he was making a mental note to talk to Keith. "Were there people there that you didn't know?" he asked.

"Of course. There always are. There were several tourists and those kinds of presentations always bring out the history buffs—at least based on the other ones we've done. I know there were a few people who came from Minneapolis. During Everett's talk I remember there were several real estate developers in the audience."

"Developers?" Marcus frowned. "Why?"

"Everett told me they showed up for one of two reasons— he was talking about old buildings in Mayville Heights and Red Wing, and developers want to know some of the history of a property they want to restore to exploit those details for financing. Or they want to know a property's past to be sure they won't face too much opposition because they want to tear it down. Do you remember that old bank building in Red Wing that was turned into condos? The plans had to be adapted because of the historical significance of the property."

Marcus rubbed the back of his neck with one hand. "How did Leitha act while she was at the library that day?"

"Like I said before, I wasn't watching the woman all the time."

"Anything you saw might be helpful."

I sighed. "You know how she could be. She had a rather superior attitude."

He nodded.

"Every time I looked in Leitha's direction while Mary was speaking, she had a look of disdain on her face. Now, if Mary noticed and if it bothered her at all, you couldn't tell. And to be fair, Leitha had acted the same way during Everett's talk, so I don't think it was personal."

"Is there anything else you can remember?"

My fingers were still linked with his. I traced my thumb along the side of his hand. "I'm not really sure what you're looking for."

He gave me a wry smile. "That makes two of us. You did say that Leitha had one of Eric's cookies. I know she drank a cup of tea at some point. According to her stomach contents, she'd had tea with milk and sugar. Was that at the library?"

"Yes," I said.

"Did she get the tea herself or did someone else get it for her?"

I knew what he was getting at. If Leitha's death hadn't been an accident, if she had died because of an overdose of potassium chloride—and I was having trouble with the idea—then maybe she had ingested it at the library.

"Someone else got it— Well, sort of."

"Wait a second. What do you mean, someone else got it 'sort of'?"

I exhaled loudly, feeling frustrated. "This is secondhand, so you should really talk to Rebecca. She told me this story the day after Leitha died." I remembered Rebecca saying she didn't like speaking ill of the dead.

"And I will," Marcus said. "Please, just tell me what you know for now."

I picked up the spoon from my frozen yogurt container and turned it over in my fingers. "As far as I know, this happened right before the argument between Leitha and Mary. Leitha did have a cup of tea, but it was actually Jonas's cup that she had taken from his hand, which according to Rebecca was her entitled way of behaving."

"Do you know if he poured the tea himself?" Marcus asked.

I nodded. "Rebecca said that he did and she remembers him drinking from it while the two of them were talking. I don't see how there could have been anything in the tea. Who could have guessed Leitha would take his cup? And anyway, Jonas is fine."

"I know," he said. "I might be completely off base about all of this but I need to be certain."

It was starting to get dark. "Are you ready to go?" Marcus

asked, gathering up both of our empty yogurt containers. We started walking back to his SUV.

"When do you expect the medical examiner will have something?" I said.

He shrugged. "I'm not sure. Maybe a week."

Actually it took fewer than three days to get some answers. On Friday, after some investigation by the police and more tests by the medical examiner, the cause of Leitha Finnamore Anderson's death was changed from accident to homicide.

chapter 11

I was sitting at the kitchen table with Owen on my lap, eating a toasted bagel topped with tomato slices when Marcus called with the news. "You were right," I said.

"It might have been better if I'd been wrong." I heard the squeak of his desk chair. "Now I have two murder cases and no idea if they're connected or not."

"You'll figure it out," I said. Owen bobbed his head seemingly in agreement. "Owen and I have faith in you."

He laughed. "Well, then, how can I go wrong?"

Midmorning I got a call from Mike Bishop's office. It was the office manager, Caroline. I'd been expecting to hear from her ever since I'd talked to Maggie.

"Hi, Kathleen," she said. "I see from our records that you were coming back for a recheck on the tooth where we did the root canal. I don't mean to push you but I was wondering what you want to do."

"I don't really know," I said, dropping onto the footstool. "What are my options?"

"Well, there are several endodontists in Minneapolis. We could forward your records to one of them and I'm sure they would check the tooth for you. Is it giving you any trouble?"

Owen came down the stairs and over to me, looking quizzically at the phone.

"It's not. I don't have any pain at all now."

"Then you'd probably be okay not having it checked. It was just something Dr. B. liked to do."

"He was very conscientious," I said.

"Yes, he was." Caroline cleared her throat. "So I could just send your records over to your regular dentist. I can tell you that we know of an endodontist who is planning on setting up a practice here in Mayville Heights, probably this winter. If you did have any problems down the road and you didn't want to drive to Minneapolis, that would be an option."

Owen jumped onto my lap and pushed his face close to the receiver. I shifted him sideways and he gave me a sour look.

"I'm not sure what to do," I said. "That tooth gave me so much trouble before the root canal—"

"You're afraid something's going to go wrong again."

"Yes," I said. "I know how silly that sounds."

"It's not silly at all," Caroline said. "I have a suggestion. Why don't you stop by the office sometime? Lorraine is here. You could ask her any questions you have. That might help you make up your mind." Lorraine was one of the dental assistants in the practice. She was kind and very reassuring.

"I could stop in on my way to the library just before lunch."

"We'll see you then," she said.

Owen looked from the phone to me as I hung up.

"I'm going to stop at Mike's office," I said. "Teeth stuff."

He made a face. Owen hated having his teeth cleaned.

"Maybe I'll learn something useful."

The cat gave a noncommittal murp and followed me out to the kitchen.

"What do you think?" I asked. "Is Marcus right? Is there some kind of connection between Mike's and Leitha's deaths or is it just one weird coincidence?"

He seemed to think about my words for a minute; then he blinked his golden eyes at me. Okay, so he wasn't sure, either.

I poured a cup of coffee, and when I turned around again, Owen was sitting on my chair, eyeing the laptop that was on the table. Roma had sent the photos from the concert and I wanted to take a look at them. Apparently, Owen did as well.

I set my coffee on the table, well away from the computer, scooped up the cat and sat down. He looked over my shoulder at the toaster and then looked at me.

"We don't need toast and peanut butter," I said.

The photos were terrific. There were two of Marcus and me

from the side. We were holding hands while I leaned against his arm. There were three of Roma and me singing along with the band, arms across each other's shoulders. In one of the shots Eddie had taken of Mary and Marcus dancing, he'd caught her in midtwirl.

"I think that's my favorite," I said, pointing at the screen.

Owen's response was to put a paw on the keyboard and suddenly we were looking at an image of Maggie. "Merow!" he said. It was clear which photo was his favorite.

Roma had included several shots of the band. I smiled as I scrolled through the pictures and felt my throat tighten over an image of Mike and Harry grinning at each other as they played.

It wasn't fair. Mike had been one of the good guys. When I got to the library, he should be there flirting with the ladies in the Seniors' Book Club and laughing about some family scandal he'd uncovered with Abigail.

"We have to find the person who did this," I said to Owen.

He nuzzled my chin. He was in.

I decided I'd eat once I got to the library, so I packed my lunch and drove down to Mike Bishop's office. Caroline was at the reception desk.

"Hi, Kathleen," she said. "I'll let Lorraine know you're here."

I took a seat in the waiting room. Lorraine appeared a couple of minutes later. She smiled when she caught sight of me.

She was short and curvy and seemed to smile all the time. She had gorgeous red curls that she generally wore in a high ponytail. Before today I didn't think I'd ever seen her in the office with her hair down.

"How are you?" I asked.

Her mouth twisted to one side. "Still a bit in shock like everyone else." She looked around. "It seems so quiet in here. I'm still having trouble with the idea that the concert was the last time I'm ever going to see Mike."

She swallowed and I reached over and put a hand on her arm for a moment.

"The concert was incredible," I said.

Lorraine's smile returned. "It's funny. That Thursday Mike was just about bouncing all around the office and I chalked it up to him being a bit wired about Johnny Rock performing again. I had no idea we were going to see the band. I can't believe he managed to keep it all secret, because trust me, he was lousy at keeping secrets."

"But we really should have guessed," Caroline said.

Lorraine and I both turned to look at her.

"What makes you say that?" I asked.

Caroline gestured at the computer. "Mike was insistent that he had to leave on time on both Wednesday and Thursday. I had to schedule anything that had the possibility of running late for earlier in the day. More than once he missed lunch to get caught up. I can't believe that it never entered my mind that the band was getting back together."

Lorraine went over my options again and I decided to have my records sent to my regular dentist for now. "I don't think you're going to have any problems with that tooth," she said, "but if you do, any of the endodontists in Minneapolis are good."

I thanked her for her help and headed for the library. Mary was at the circulation desk. I hadn't seen her in a couple of days.

"You're early," she said.

I held up the cooler bag. "I had a stop to make, so I thought I'd have lunch here. Maybe out in the gazebo." I pulled out my phone and brought up the photos of her and Marcus. "Eddie took these," I said. "Roma is going to send you copies."

"I look pretty good," Mary said. "And that guy of yours is a real hottie."

I felt my cheeks getting red. "I'm just going to pretend you didn't say that," I said.

Mary laughed; then her expression became serious. "I heard the news about Leitha Anderson's death. And I've already talked to Marcus."

"Was there really anyone who would have wanted Leitha dead? I know she was—"

"Arrogant, rude, condescending?" Mary finished. "A lot of people might have wished she wasn't around, but as far as actually killing her? I don't think so. There's a big difference between wishing someone were dead and actually making it happpen." She picked up a pen and tapped it on the desk.

"Leitha just had a way of getting under people's skin. The day she was here, the day she died, she was annoyed at me because I could show the Finnamores had very little to do with settling the town. And Lordy, she was constantly nitpicking with Mike when he was alive because she wanted him to settle down and make little Finnamore babies."

"Do you think it bothered him?" I asked.

Mary gave a snort of laughter. "Not in the slightest. I remember her complaining that he didn't think about how his choices in his personal life affected her. She was always disappointed because Jonas wasn't a biological Finnamore—or as she put it, a 'real' Finnamore—like anyone cared. Before she died she was even butting in on where Lachlan was going to go to college and what he was going to study."

"It really mattered to her?"

"You'd better believe it did," she said, tapping the pen again for emphasis. "She wanted him to go into medicine or business, which is what the Finnamore men do. The Finnamore name and its legacy were the most important things to Leitha. From what I've heard, it was the same way with Leitha's grandfather, so she got it honestly. The two disappointments in the family were Mike working on people's teeth and Jonas becoming a college professor and PhD. Those were *not* the career paths she had chosen for them."

I shook my head. "It sounds exhausting."

"I think in some ways it was more exhausting for her."

"What happened to Lachlan's parents," I asked. "I know

they were killed in an accident but I don't know any of the details."

Mary shook her head. "That was before you got here. It was heartbreaking. They were on their way back from Minneapolis and hit a patch of black ice that spun them into the path of a furniture delivery truck. Colin was killed outright. The driver of the truck and Ainsley were badly injured. The truck driver had to have his left leg amputated below the knee, but he did recover. Ainsley spent months in a coma before she died. Lachlan was just eleven. Luckily, he had stayed with Jonas. And I have to give credit where credit is due, for all of Leitha's abrasive ways, she rallied around the child just the way everyone else did."

It was good to hear the woman had had a heart after all. I hadn't really seen that.

I dropped my things in my office and had my lunch outside in the gazebo. Marcus called to say he was on his way to Minneapolis to talk to the doctor heading the cardiac study again.

"I don't know when I'll get back," he said.

"I love you," I said. "Drive safe."

I wasn't that hungry when I got home, so I toasted another bagel, cut a slice of cheddar and poured a glass of lemonade, promising myself I'd eat extra vegetables tomorrow.

The house felt warm and stuffy. I took my food and the laptop and went to sit in the backyard. I was halfway through my bagel, looking at the concert photos again when Hercules came though the porch door. Literally. He walked across the grass, sat at my feet and meowed. I patted my lap. "You can come up."

He meowed again.

"You're perfectly capable of jumping," I said. "It's not that far."

He still didn't move.

"I guess you don't want a bit of cheese, then."

He was on my lap almost before I got the words out, his black-and-white face looming in front of mine. I broke off a tiny bite of cheese and handed it to him. He murped a thank-you and ate it. Then he poked at my legs until he was settled in to look at the computer screen with me.

I scrolled through the photos so the cat could see all of them and I told him about my visit to Mike's office and about what I'd learned from Mary. He tipped his head to one side as though he were thinking about everything I'd said. Then he swiped a paw at the touch pad and a shot of Mike and Harry filled the screen. He turned to look at me as though he expected me to do or say something.

I studied the photo but saw nothing that would help figure out who had killed Mike. "I know you're not trying to suggest that Harry is the killer, so I don't see what you want me to see," I said.

I moved on to one of the images of Roma and me, arms over each other's shoulders. When I took a drink from my lemonade, Hercules managed to go back to the photo of Harry and Mike. I had a cat with computer skills that were better than those some people had.

I narrowed my gaze at him. "Quit it!" I said.

He gave a huff of impatience.

I broke the last little piece of cheese in half and gave one piece to him. I ate the other one. "Sometimes I wish you could talk," I said.

He made an indignant meow.

"Talk in a language I understand, I mean." I looked at the image on the laptop and thought about how much fun Mike and Harry had been having that night and how magical it had been to be there.

Hercules peered into my lemonade, wrinkled his nose and then began to wash his face, shooting looks at the computer and me from time to time. Whatever I was supposed to see, I didn't. Or maybe the cat wasn't trying to show me anything.

"The guys worked so hard to make it a surprise," I said. "And if anyone did guess, those people kept it to themselves."

"I'm pretty sure the old man figured it out, although he said he didn't," Harry had said when he'd told me about Mike being out at the house every Thursday night for weeks. "Monday through Wednesday he worked later at the office and Friday night he was checking out new music somewhere in the area. . . . Eventually, we worked things out so the others could join in on Zoom."

Johnny had told me how odd it felt not to be getting together online with the others anymore on Thursday nights.

Thursday. Not Wednesday. *Thursday.*

"That's not what Caroline told me," I said slowly.

Hercules paused the face washing with one paw in midair. It almost seemed as though there was a look of anticipation on his face.

"Mike was insistent that he had to leave on time on Wednesday and Thursday. I had to schedule anything that had the possibility of running late for earlier in the day." That's what Caroline said: *Wednesday* and Thursday.

Hercules made a soft "mrr," glanced at the screen and went back to washing his face with a murp. Had I stumbled on what he'd been trying to tell me?

A moth fluttered by only a couple of inches from the cat's face. He leaped into the air, lost his balance and landed awkwardly—albeit upright—on the lawn. He gave himself a shake and looked kind of embarrassed. The moth was fine.

Was it possible that Mike Bishop was doing something on Wednesday nights that he didn't want anyone to know about? I knew I needed to check with Harry and maybe the rest of the band to make sure he hadn't been practicing on Wednesdays, too. Was I on to something? Or was my leap of logic as ungainly as Herc's leap after that moth? Had Mike had a secret of his own?

chapter 12

I decided that I would call Harry once the library closed for the day, but when I pulled into the parking lot Saturday morning, his truck was already there and he was unloading the lawn mower.

"I thought I'd get an early start," he said. His mouth worked as though he were trying out what he wanted to say before he actually said the words. "Kathleen, I don't mean to push but I just wondered if you've come up with anything yet."

I knew he meant about Mike's killer.

"I'm sorry," I said. "I haven't. Not yet, but I do have a question. Did you and Mike ever practice on Wednesday?"

He shook his head. "As far as I know, he was at the office getting caught up with paperwork on Wednesday nights. That's what he said."

"Could he have been getting together with someone else to rehearse?"

"Not with Paul. He had something going on with his kids on Wednesdays. I can check with Ritchie and Johnny if that will help."

"I'll talk to Johnny myself," I said. "But if you could ask Ritchie, that would help."

"What does this have to do with who killed Mike?"

I shrugged. "At this point I don't know."

"Okay," he said. "I'll see what I can find out and I'll talk to you later. I'll be out this afternoon to do the mowing and clipping at your place and I'll take a look at the problem with the downspout."

I thanked him and went inside.

About half an hour later, as I was wrestling with a shelf that seemed to be permanently stuck at a thirty-degree angle, Maggie called to invite me to join her and Roma for a late lunch at Eric's. I was already feeling frustrated and too warm. Lunch that I didn't have to make sounded wonderful. "I'll walk over right after we close," I said.

When the mail arrived on Friday, I had found the copy of the map I'd requested for Mike along with a note from the reference librarian in Grand Rapids. I called Jonas to let him know he could come and get the map along with the copies of the census. I'd also found a zippered folder of notes and papers that Mike had left behind. Everything was in my office sitting on my desk.

I had expected to get Jonas's voice mail but I got him instead.

"I'm free at the moment," he said. "Would it be all right if I came over now?"

"Of course," I said. "I'll see you soon."

Jonas walked in about half an hour later, just as I was pushing an empty book cart back to the front desk. He was wearing jeans and a gray T-shirt and something about the measured way he moved made me think of Lachlan. They didn't really look like they were related. Lachlan had the Finnamore green eyes while Jonas's eyes were dark. Jonas kept his wavy hair short, while Lachlan's hair brushed his shoulders when it wasn't pulled back in a ponytail. Like Mike, Lachlan was very animated when he spoke, but his Quinn DNA showed in the way he moved.

"Everything is in my office," I said. "C'mon up with me."

He followed me up the stairs. I unlocked my office door and picked up the folder and the file of papers from my desk. I handed everything to Jonas.

He stared at the papers for a moment before he took them from me. "Is . . . is this everything?" he asked.

"As far as I know. I think the last time Mike was here, he

was in a bit of a rush. It was the day of the concert. That's probably why that folder got left behind, but if I find anything else, I'll set it aside and call you."

"I appreciate that," he said. "Mike and Lachlan were close and I like to think all this information about his family may be important to Lachlan someday."

"I hope it will," I said. "Mike shared a few of the stories with me. The Finnamores are a very colorful family."

He gave me a gentle smile. "That's a very diplomatic way to put things, Kathleen."

"I'm serious. For example, it turns out there's more than one musician in the family tree. An eighteenth-century bagpiper among others."

"I always said Mike had music in his blood. I guess he did. That night at the Last Bash he was so happy."

"Did you have any hint that the band was getting back together?" I asked.

His gaze softened. "I didn't. I was oblivious. There were a couple of times that Lachlan invited Mike for supper and he couldn't come, but he just said he was working late and I didn't think twice about it. That wasn't unusual. Mike was either working, out somewhere listening to live music or lately working on the family tree."

"How's Lachlan doing?"

He took off his glasses and rubbed the bridge of his nose. "Losing Mike was horrible and now learning that Leitha's death wasn't an accident . . . it's a lot for anyone to deal with.

I'm not saying she wasn't a difficult person, but we have so little family left that any loss is painful. I don't mean to put you on the spot, but do you know if Detective Gordon has any suspects, or are you even allowed to answer that?"

I wanted to give Jonas some kind of hope that the person or people who had devastated his family would be brought to justice, but I didn't know what I could say that would do that. "At this point the police are still gathering information and asking questions. I know it's probably not much comfort, but they need to be slow and meticulous so they don't miss anything that might be important."

He nodded. "Leitha was a prickly person who said what she thought, whether or not it was thoughtful or kind or helpful. She made her share of enemies over the years, but she pretty much outlived them all. You saw her argument with Mary Lowe?"

"I did."

"At the time she was annoyed at Mike over something. I don't even remember what now. I was on her good side. In a few days Mike would have gotten back on the A-list and I would likely have been on the naughty list, so to speak, once again. It was just the way Leitha was in her personal life as well as in business. I don't think she cared what people thought of her."

"She was a woman in the business world when it wasn't that common," I said, treading carefully because I didn't want to offend Jonas. "She must have developed a thick skin."

"Like a rhinoceros hide." He smiled to take the sting out of his words. "As a young woman, Leitha worked with her grandfather at Black Dog and over time she built up a small portfolio of properties that she was still very hands-on with right up until she died. In fact, she had a potential deal with Everett Henderson that had fallen apart just before her death—I don't know any of the details—and I'm not trying to suggest that Everett had anything to do with her death."

He paused, almost as though he was weighing what he wanted to say next. "Kathleen, I hope I'm not being, well, rude, but I know you have some experience in this kind of thing. Do you think it's possible that Leitha's death and Mike's death are somehow connected? I thought that Mike had walked in on someone in the middle of breaking in to his house."

I shifted uneasily from one foot to the other. The conversation made me uncomfortable. I understood that Jonas wanted answers but I wasn't the person who could give them to him. "I think it's way too soon to know at this point."

"I admit I'm still having trouble with the idea that Leitha's death wasn't an accident. I keep thinking that maybe she took the potassium chloride by accident or even by design, not realizing it could hurt her. She did seem to be getting a bit fatigued on occasion, but she was in her nineties. She was very private about her health along with everything else. It was her generation. Now I wish that I'd pushed."

I gave him what I hoped was a reassuring smile. "From

what I knew of Leitha, I don't think pushing would have worked with her."

Jonas nodded. "Her response to being pushed was to push back even harder."

"Give the police time, Jonas," I said. "They're good at what they do."

"You're right," he said. "Thank you for listening and for all of this." He held up the papers.

"If I find anything else, I'll be in touch," I said.

Jonas left and I sat down at my desk and looked at the phone. I didn't think for a moment that Everett had had anything to do with Leitha's death, but I was curious about their failed deal. I decided to call Henderson Holdings and leave a message for Lita. To my surprise she answered the phone.

"Hi. I didn't expect to actually get you," I said when she picked up.

She laughed. "That begs the question: Then why did you call?"

"I was going to leave a message."

"You can still do that if you want to," she teased. "I just came in to clean up a few things from yesterday that had to be put aside because the power went out. I only picked up because I recognized the number and guessed it was you. What do you need?"

"Information," I said. There was no need to beat around the bush with Lita.

"That I have. Whether or not it's the information you're looking for, I can't say."

"Tell me about the deal between Everett and Leitha Anderson."

She didn't ask why I wanted to know. "Leitha owned a property in Red Wing that Everett was interested in turning into condos or apartments."

"It's something he's done before."

"Oh yes, restoring an old building instead of tearing it down." Like Mary and Harrison, Everett cared about the history of the state, and as he'd said at his presentation, not every old structure could be saved or should be, but they shouldn't all be torn down, either. "You know how Everett—and Rebecca—feel about not losing our ties to the past."

"'A people without the knowledge of their past history, origin and culture is like a tree without roots,'" I said. "Marcus Garvey."

"Mr. Garvey was a very wise man," Lita said.

I propped an elbow on my desk and leaned the side of my head against my hand. "So what made the project fall apart?"

"Leitha's pigheadedness. John Stone came to see Everett. He wanted to buy that building himself. John believed it had been the home of the first music school in the state, predating the MacPhail School by about two years. He wanted to turn the property back into a school. Everett agreed and tried to convince Leitha to sell to John instead."

"I take it that didn't go well."

"No, it did not," she said emphatically. "Leitha didn't like John. I don't think she ever liked the idea of Mike being in the band. She found that kind of thing unseemly for a Finnamore man. So she didn't want to be accommodating. And she saw John's desire to save the building as nothing more than just foolish sentimentality. Those were her exact words, 'foolish sentimentality.'"

The same expression she'd used with me about renovating the library.

"She decided to sell to someone else who was going to tear down the building and turn it into a parking lot. John was furious and Everett wasn't too happy, either."

"There was nothing either of them could do?" I asked.

"No. Leitha and Everett had no agreement in place on the property. And it was impossible to reason with her. It was weeks before John got over his anger. Finally, he just seemed to accept there was nothing he could do. He even told Everett to let it go."

"That's not exactly something Everett is good at."

Lita laughed. "No, it isn't." There was silence for a moment. "Kathleen, I heard that the police think Leitha's death wasn't an accident after all. Does any of this have anything to do with that building?"

I shook my head even though she wasn't there to see me. "I honestly don't know."

"Well, if you think any of this will help Marcus, go ahead and tell him. He knows where to find us if he has any questions."

"I will. Thank you," I said.

After we hung up, I got to my feet and went to stand by the window. I looked out over the water. It occurred to me that to solve one murder, I might just have to solve two.

chapter 13

I spent the rest of the morning shelving books and helping several people find something new to read. The latter was one of my favorite parts of the job. It always made my day when I suggested a book to someone and they came back to tell me that they had enjoyed it.

I discovered that someone had put gum on three different shelves in the reference section. Grape-flavored bubble gum, it seemed.

I rubbed the space between my eyebrows. "Some days I think gum should be a controlled substance," I muttered to Levi, who had been helping me get the reference section back to rights. Several students who were taking a summer school history class had just spent the last hour looking for references in "real" books for a class assignment.

"Did you know that the ancient Greeks chewed gum?" Levi asked.

"I did not," I said. "And I hope none of those ancient Greeks ever stuck their gum on one of the wings on the statue of Nike or on Venus de Milo's shoulder."

He laughed. Then he gestured at the shelf. "I can take care of that," he said.

"Are you sure?" I asked. Getting gum off anything was a tedious job. I thought about Mariah doing the same thing out at the diner.

"It's no problem," Levi said.

"You'll need a scraper. That stuff sticks like superglue. It took forever to get it out of the book drop."

"I used to be a room service waiter, remember? Everywhere someone can put gum, I've probably seen. Including some that, trust me, you don't want to know about."

He headed upstairs to get the scraper and I thought once again how glad I was that I'd hired Levi. The senior ladies loved his manners and were always bringing cookies to try to fatten him up. He had very wide tastes in reading material, which meant he could help pretty much any reader find something they'd like, and he knew more about graphic novels than I did.

I went back to the front desk to get the last cart of books to put on the shelves.

"You don't want Levi to finish this?" Abigail asked.

"He's scraping gum off one of the shelves."

She shook her head. "I swear some people behave like they were raised by wolves."

"I don't think wolves chew gum," I said.

"Then they clearly have better manners than some of our patrons."

I smiled. "No argument here."

Abigail had been on tour for her most recent children's book in June. She had a contract to write three more books in the series and I wondered sometimes if we'd lose her to a full-time career as a writer. She was very talented. I suspected her main character—a daring little girl with five bossy older brothers— was modeled after the little girl Abigail herself once was. She, too, had five older brothers. She'd even created a secret code so she could write things in what she called her logbook and they wouldn't be able to read it.

The first day she was back at work—which happened to be a Friday—Mike had come in with coffee and muffins for the whole staff, but I'd always had the feeling the gesture was really aimed at Abigail. I'd harbored a secret hope that the two of them might get together. Now that was never going to happen.

Maggie and Roma were already at a table when I got to Eric's Place. "Have you been waiting very long?" I asked as I slid onto my chair.

"I just got here," Roma said.

"And I barely got here before she got here," Maggie added.

Claire came over to take our orders. We all decided on the chopped salad and breadsticks. "And how about the blackberry iced tea?" Claire suggested. She smiled at me. "I know it's not coffee, Kathleen, but I think you'll like it."

"I'll try it," Maggie said.

Roma nodded. "Me too."

They all looked at me.

"So will I," I said.

"Seriously?" Roma said. She looked . . . surprised.

"I do drink more than coffee." Even I could hear that I sounded a little defensive.

"Not very often," Maggie teased.

Claire gathered our menus. "If you don't like it, I'll bring you coffee, I promise," she whispered as she collected mine.

"I heard about the medical examiner reclassifying Leitha Anderson's death," Roma said, picking up her napkin.

"Marcus doesn't think her death is connected to Mike's, does he?" Maggie asked.

I wasn't sure how to answer. I didn't want to say that he did and I was beginning think he might be right. "As far as I know they're two separate cases." I was saved from having to say anything more because Claire came back with the iced tea, which was as good as she had said it would be.

"How's hockey school going?" I asked once Claire had

headed to another table. I was genuinely interested and I didn't want to talk about Mike or Leitha right now.

"It's going very well," Roma said. "Eddie is a natural teacher and he's already getting phone calls from high school and college hockey teams looking to work with him."

Despite all the obstacles he'd encountered in getting the school up and running, and despite people telling him he should set up in Minneapolis, Eddie had never wavered from running his hockey school in his new hometown.

"Maybe I should get him to give me skating lessons," I said, reaching for my glass. I had never learned to skate as a kid. Both Maggie and Marcus had tried to teach me. All I'd managed to learn was how to fall so I didn't break anything.

"He would, you know," Roma said. "I should have thought of that a long time ago."

"You're good at standing up," Maggie offered. She always managed to find something positive to say.

"I'm fantastic at standing up," I said. "It's just moving that stymies me."

"Talk to Eddie," Roma said. "I'm serious. He'll teach you."

"I will," I said. I took another sip of my iced tea.

Roma put both of her hands flat on the table. "Before Claire comes back, I have to confess. I had an ulterior motive for suggesting we have lunch. I need both of your opinions on something."

"We are full of opinions," I said solemnly, squaring my shoulders and laying one hand on my chest.

Maggie nodded in agreement, looking equally serious.

Roma gave her head a little shake. "The two of you are full of something."

Mags smiled at her. "How can we help?"

"Do you remember the burlesque show at The Brick that raised money for the no-kill shelter?"

Maggie's eyes met mine and she grinned.

"Vividly," I said. "Mary put on a push to get me to take part in it."

Maggie was still grinning. "You should have said yes. It looked like a lot of fun."

I squinted across the table at her. "I don't remember seeing you on that stage."

"Mary didn't ask me, but I would have if I'd had the chance."

"You might want to be careful about saying that in front of witnesses," Roma said.

"Why?" I asked, unfolding my napkin and putting it in my lap.

"Because there may be another show."

Maggie eyed her, the remnants of a grin still on her face. "You're serious," she said.

Roma nodded. "Very."

At that moment Claire returned with our food. Once we all had our salads and fat, chewy breadsticks, I turned to Roma. "Another show? Explain please."

"I thought the original show was supposed to strictly be a

onetime thing. Basically a last-minute idea to help raise enough money to fix the roof at the no-kill shelter," Maggie added.

"It was," Roma said. "I don't know if you remember, but we were desperate. The roof was leaking in about a dozen places and none of the other fund-raising efforts were bringing in the kind of money we needed. Mary suggested a burlesque-style show—nothing that involved nudity or anything obscene, just a little slightly naughty fun. She convinced The Brick to give us the stage for a night and to kick in a percentage of the drink totals."

Mary might look like someone's kindly cookie-baking grandmother, but she was also an example of the old saying that looks could be deceiving. She was the state kickboxing champion in her age group and she danced regularly at amateur night at The Brick. Like the burlesque show, there was no nudity, just fishnets, feathers and flirtation.

In the weeks before the first show, I'd learned a lot about burlesque from Mary. She'd explained that shows usually featured a master of ceremonies whose job it was to keep the show moving forward. The MC not only introduced each act; he or she also interacted with the audience. Most acts ran five minutes or less. The performers included dancers, singers, magicians, comedians and, yes, striptease artists.

"But not in this show, I promise," Mary had said when my eyebrows went up, "although . . ." She'd winked and given me a sly smile.

Mary had used all of her persuasive skills to try to get me to take part in the fund-raiser. "First of all, I don't dance," I had told her. "And second, I'm not the kind of person to put on fishnets and feathers."

"Everyone can dance," she'd retorted, "and fishnets and feathers are flattering to every body type."

In burlesque everything was big: lots of makeup, lots of hair, especially wigs, and costumes that were detailed and elaborate. There were rhinestones and sequins on everything. Burlesque, I discovered, was intended to make the audience laugh. It poked fun and skewered people and ideas alike.

We had sold tickets at the library in advance and they were available at the door as well. People were also encouraged to sponsor a cat. There were posters all over the bar on the day of the show. Ticket sales had been decent but donations to sponsor cats were slow despite the fact that the audience was clearly having a lot of fun.

Then Zorro came out. The lights went down and the theme song from the 1950s show began to play; then the music changed to a dance mix.

No one knew who the man was, but he put on the performance of a lifetime. He was bare chested under a satiny cape with black leggings and what looked to me to be black Docs. A silky bandanna with eyeholes covered the top of his face and his hair. He also wore a black hat. And he'd gotten a genuine fencing foil from somewhere. What he lacked in skill, he more than made up for with his enthusiasm.

Most of the time it's not acceptable to call out to a performer while they're in the middle of their act or to whistle at them from the back. With burlesque, it's expected. The audience doesn't have to wait to politely clap at the end. They're expected to show how they feel during the performance with comments, whistles, claps and screams of laughter. That audience loved Zorro. People laughed but because they were having fun, not at his expense. As he left the stage, the crowd erupted in even louder applause, hooting and stomping their feet.

Mary came out and promised another dance from the masked man when they reached a certain dollar value in sponsorships. It worked. The masked man danced again at the end of the evening and the event surpassed its goal. Since then Mary had refused to give even a hint as to the man's identity. I knew I had a better chance of finding out the secret ingredient in her cinnamon rolls.

I pulled my attention back to the current conversation.

Roma speared a chunk of cucumber with her fork. "You know the shelter never really has enough money, not for long-term things like work on the building."

Maggie and I both nodded.

"Well, about a month ago, Sandra mentioned in passing that we should do another show—maybe make it an annual thing—to raise money for the shelter."

Sandra Godfrey was a mail carrier. She was *my* mail carrier. She was also a member of the library board, which was how she'd gotten to be friends with Mary.

"I've been thinking about the idea on and off since she mentioned it," Roma continued. "And it strikes me that maybe it's not such a bad idea. What do you two think?"

"I think you should do it," Maggie said, gesturing with her fork. "I'm not sure if The Brick is the best venue, though. You might get a larger audience if you held the show somewhere else."

"I thought about that," Roma said. "There are other possibilities." She looked at me.

"I'm sorry, not the library," I said.

She and Maggie laughed. "No, not the library, but what do you think about the idea?"

"I think it could work. Could you get enough performers?"

Roma grinned. "Well, apparently Maggie is in."

Maggie looked up from her salad. "I am."

"Sandra has really taken to the dancing since Mary got her started. She's done more than one workshop herself and she's been teaching a few women the art of erotic dancing over the past few months. I don't think there would be a problem getting enough participants."

"What, no would-be Zorros?" Maggie asked.

"Maggie's right," I said. "If you could get Zorro again, whoever he was, that would be a big draw."

"I think it was Burtis," Maggie said.

"Did Brady say something to you?" I asked.

She shook her head and her blond curls bounced. "No, but Burtis does love animals and the body type was right."

I held up one hand. "No, no, no. I don't want to think about Burtis in a cape. Now that's going to be in my head all day."

"What about Thorsten?" Roma asked.

Maggie wrinkled her nose. "Too tall."

"Maybe Everett?"

Even I had to laugh at that suggestion. I couldn't imagine Everett dancing in a mask and a cape. "I'm not going there," I said. "I have to work with the man and I don't want to be in a meeting and suddenly find myself wondering if that was him in that cape and mask. Besides, I don't believe Rebecca would have been able to keep the secret from everyone."

Maggie and Roma continued to speculate as I spotted Eric and got up to talk to him. "I'll be right back," I said.

Eric smiled when he caught sight of me walking toward him. "How are you?" he said. "I haven't seen you since the funeral."

"I'm well, thank you. I wanted to thank you for sending the extra cookies from the service over for the Reading Club kids. They were a big hit."

Eric smiled. "Hey, no problem. There were two plates that didn't even have the tops removed and I didn't want to see them go to waste. And you know Mike was a softie when it came to kids. I figured he'd be happy that they got the leftovers." He looked away for a moment and then his gaze came back to me. "It's funny, you know. He was in here a lot in the weeks before he died. I keep expecting to see him come through the door, telling me he needs the largest cup of coffee I have."

"I know what you mean," I said. "Mike was at the library working on his family tree. I keep expecting to come around a corner and see him at a table with a stack of reference books."

"He told me about that. He'd come in after work every Wednesday for takeout, and if it wasn't busy, we'd talk for a few minutes. I didn't think of it at the time, but it's clear in retrospect that he was going to practice with the rest of the band." He shook his head. "Marcus is going to catch whoever did this, right?"

"He's doing his best," I said. "Hold a good thought."

We talked for a minute or two longer and then I went back to the table. So Mike had been getting takeout every Wednesday night. Eric's words matched what Caroline had told me. Mike had been doing something on Wednesday nights. I had no idea what it was but he'd definitely had a secret. Had it gotten him killed?

chapter 14

I went back to the table to find that Maggie and Roma had given up trying to figure out who Zorro was and were now trying to pick a piece of music for Maggie to dance to if there was in fact another show.

"And I think you should give Sandra a call," Roma was saying as I sat down again. "You could have a couple of lessons so you'd feel more comfortable onstage."

After lunch we parted company on the sidewalk in front of the café. Maggie had a shift at the artists' co-op store and Roma was on her way over to take lunch to Eddie. I hugged them both.

"You know, Sandra does take students for one-on-one lessons," Roma teased. "I mean, if you happen to be interested."

"You're as persistent as Owen," I said.

"Since I know the little furball, I'm going to take that as a compliment," she said with a grin

"I don't dance. I'll hang posters. I'll sell tickets. I'll help make costumes. *I'm not dancing.*"

"Put her down as a maybe," Maggie said. She grabbed Roma by the arm and pulled her down the sidewalk. I could hear them both laughing.

I was meeting Marcus at the bookstore in a little while. Mary had told him about a book on forgotten landmarks in the state that he wanted to get for his father. Since I knew Marcus should be there in less than half an hour, I decided to take a walk along the Riverwalk. It was too nice a day to go back to my office and do paperwork.

I hadn't gone very far when I saw Johnny coming toward me. He smiled when he saw me. "I thought I was the only person who didn't find it too warm to be out walking," he said as we got closer to each other.

"The Riverwalk is one of my favorite places," I said. "I did a lot of walking here when I first came to town. I'd go all the way to Wild Rose Bluff and back sometimes."

"I've been walking down by the marina. Mike and I were working on a song and I keep going back there, hoping inspiration will hit so I can finish it."

"I'm sure it will," I said.

"I'm glad I saw you," Johnny said. "I'm looking for some information on a former music academy in Red Wing. I'm hoping you might know of a reference book that could help."

"You mean the property you tried to buy from Leitha."

"Yes." He looked a little surprised that I knew. "Kathleen, I'm angry about Mike's death. So angry some days I could punch someone, which wouldn't do me or anyone else any good. But I'm not sorry Leitha is dead and I won't be a hypocrite and pretend I am now that it seems her death wasn't an accident."

"Leitha brought out strong feelings in a lot of people," I said, matching his quiet tone.

"Very diplomatic," he said.

"It doesn't make the words any less true."

"She was managing to estrange her whole family. Her daughter had very little to do with her. In fact she moved to the other side of the country. Lachlan avoided Leitha as much as he could and she and Mike were on the outs when she died but Mike didn't even know what over. It's hard to feel grief-stricken over someone who alienated so many people. Mike on the other hand, that wasn't fair."

I shook my head. "No, it wasn't."

I could hear my mother's voice in my head saying, *Life is not always fair, Katydid. Sometimes bad people win. Sometimes good people lose.*

"She tried to sabotage your project." We started walking back the way I'd just come.

"She went out of her way to try to make sure it didn't happen. I offered her a good price for the property—ten percent over Everett's offer and his was more than fair. But that wasn't the only reason I didn't like her," he said. "I didn't like the way she was always trying to interfere in Lachlan's life. He's a good kid."

It was impossible not to hear the intensity in his voice and see the angry lines pulling at his mouth.

"I know she had some pretty rigid ideas about what he should do with his life."

"In her mind there was a very limited list of careers for Finnamore men and anything related to music was out. I think Lachlan could have said he wanted to play for the Chicago Symphony Orchestra or the Berlin Philharmonic, and that wouldn't have satisfied her. Jonas put up with way too much of her meddling and threats to hold back money for Lachlan's college education. I like the guy, but he's always been too much of a soft touch. I think he should have stood up to her. He always said he wanted to make sure that Leitha wouldn't be able to interfere with Lachlan getting his money for college. I told him more than once that he should have told her to stuff her Finnamore money. Lachlan is really talented. Even if the old crab had somehow managed to hold back the trust money, Lachlan could get a scholarship."

I'd had no idea Johnny had so much animosity for Leitha. In a moment of anger, could he have done something stupid? I didn't want to believe it.

"You know I was at the library for the presentation the day of Leitha's accident," Johnny said. "I guess I shouldn't say 'accident' anymore."

"I remember seeing you." I wanted to ask him what he was getting at, but I'd learned that if I just let people talk, sometimes I found out more than if I asked a lot of questions. It took patience I didn't always have.

"Mary wasn't the only person who had words with Leitha." He exhaled loudly. "I did as well. It was the same old conversation about not letting me buy that building. She took great pleasure in telling me that she had sold the property to another developer."

"You must have been angry," I said.

He shrugged. "Some days you eat the bear. Some days the bear eats you. And so far the building is still standing, so you never know what might happen."

The intensity that had been in his voice earlier was gone and the lines in his face had smoothed out. Why was he so calm now about something that had left him so angry when Leitha was alive? Leitha meddling in her great-great-nephew's life had gotten more of a reaction from Johnny than that deal that had fallen through.

Johnny suddenly smiled. "We got tattoos, you know," he said, "about a week before Leitha died."

"You and Mike?" I didn't see Harry going to get a tattoo. On the other hand, I'd been learning that Harry had layers I didn't know about.

"Yeah," he said. "Nothing wild. Just the sign language symbol for rock and roll." He touched his left hip. "I have no idea how but Leitha found out. You can imagine how she reacted. Mike didn't give a sh— Mike didn't care. She blamed me. Mike told her it was his idea. She wouldn't hear it."

"But it was your idea, wasn't it?"

He grinned. "Oh yeah!"

We stopped by a bench at the spot where I'd first crossed the street to reach the Riverwalk trail. I gave Johnny the name of the reference librarian in Red Wing. "They have an excellent collection of old photographs. I think it's the first place you should start to try to document the building's history. I'll call her on Monday and tell her to expect to hear from you."

"Thanks, Kathleen," Johnny said. "I appreciate this."

"This is probably going to sound a little odd, but do you know what Mike was doing on Wednesday night for the last few months?" I asked.

"As far as I know, working late, having supper and this time of year watching the Twins play on TV." His eyes narrowed. "Why?"

"He'd been leaving the office on time on Wednesday and Thursday but he was only practicing on Thursday."

He shrugged. "So? Maybe he was seeing someone or maybe he just wanted to watch the ball game with a beer."

Something over my shoulder caught Johnny's eye and his face darkened. "You can't honestly think it had anything to do with Mike's death. Mike wasn't the kind of person to have secrets." He raised his voice. "And if the police were working harder instead of manufacturing cases, maybe they'd have his killer by now."

Marcus joined us, putting a hand on my back. "We are working hard on Mike's case," he said, his face devoid of emotion.

"Well, from my perspective, you seem to be spending all your efforts on Leitha Anderson's death, which no one even knew was a crime. You're wasting your time going down that road."

"Leitha deserves justice just as much as Mike does," Marcus said. "And I'm going to keep working so that they both get it."

"Mike Bishop didn't have an enemy in the world." Johnny's voice was getting angrier. "Mike made friends everywhere he went, unlike Leitha. He was ten times the person she was." He stood with his feet apart, hands jammed in his pockets. "There were some break-ins and some vandalism to cars in the area of Mike's house. Are you trying to find those people? Why aren't you checking out people who got out of prison recently? Or known drug addicts?"

I lifted a hand to touch Johnny's arm and then thought better of it. "Marcus knows how to do his job," I said gently.

He didn't look at me. "Then do it," he said, his gaze locked on Marcus's face.

"I am," Marcus said. "I'm not going to insult you by telling you to trust me, but I am looking into all of those things. And more. I give you my word."

Johnny couldn't have known how serious a promise that was, but I did.

Johnny swiped a hand over his face. The anger seemed to drain out of him. "All I care about is bringing Mike's killer to justice."

Marcus nodded. "I get that. I want the same thing. But I have to put just as much effort in for everyone. Otherwise the whole system falls apart."

They stared at each other for a long moment; then Johnny turned to me. "Thank you for the information," he said. He turned and headed across the grass.

"'Justice cannot be for one side alone, but must be for both,'" I said in a quiet voice. I knew Marcus would agree with Eleanor Roosevelt's words.

I watched Johnny cross the street and head into Eric's. I turned back to Marcus. "Did it look as though Mike had walked in on a robbery, just between us?"

He shook his head. "It did look to me as though someone might have gone through his desk. Or maybe he was just someone who had a messy desk. What bothers me is, why was he killed? If Mike had walked in on someone, why not run? None of the break-ins and vandalism out there have been anything other than stupid kids showing off, not someone who would try to rob someone's house and then kill the owner when he surprised them. And Mike was an average middle-aged person, not some big muscular guy or a martial arts expert. Killing him seems like an overreaction when it would have been so much easier to run."

"Maybe the person couldn't get away," I said.

"If Mike had come in the front door to the house, the thief could have gone out through the kitchen or through the French doors to the deck. Someone who was looking for a few dollars or something to sell would have panicked and gotten the hell out. It doesn't make sense."

That was the problem. Everywhere I turned, nothing about this case made sense.

chapter 15

There's something I need to tell you," I said. "I'm not sure if it's important or not."

"Okay. What is it?"

"Wednesday nights, Mike was making sure to leave work on time."

"Because he was going out to Harry's to practice."

I shook my head. "No, he wasn't. They practiced on Thursday. I checked with Harry."

"So he was probably just going home."

We headed for the street.

"I don't think so," I said. "He stopped at Eric's for takeout on those Wednesday nights. I don't think he was going home."

Marcus frowned. "So you think he was doing what? Leading some kind of secret life?"

"No. Maybe." It sounded silly when he said the words out loud.

"I don't think so," Marcus said. "I'm not saying your instincts aren't good, but so far from what I've learned, Mike Bishop's life was an open book."

"I hope you're right," I said.

We walked over to the bookstore and got the book for Elliot and then headed to Marcus's house. The plan was to do some yard work and figure out a permanent spot for the bench he'd bought.

I changed my clothes and started weeding the vegetable garden. Micah perched on one corner of the raised bed, watching me, while Marcus tried to decide on the best location for the bench.

"I thought you were going to paint it first," I said.

"I am," he said as he stood in the middle of the yard, looking around. "I just want to know where it's going to go when I'm finished."

I didn't follow the logic. "Okay." I looked at Micah, who seemed to shrug.

"What do you think?"

"On the deck," I said.

Micah meowed her agreement.

Marcus looked around the yard again. "I think by the rosebushes," he said, muscling the bench over the grass into place.

"Bees," I said.

He thought for a moment, then moved the bench to the other side of the bed I was working in. Micah and I exchanged another look, which this time he saw.

"What?"

I hesitated.

"You don't think this is a good spot? Why?"

"It's not a big deal. It's just that the ground is kind of uneven right there."

He pushed at one end of the seat. "There. I've found a level spot."

"Good," I said without looking up. I knew there were no level spots on that part of the lawn.

Marcus dropped onto the bench. It immediately canted sideways, almost knocking him to the ground. Micah walked around the edge of the vegetable bed, peered at Marcus and gave a concerned meow.

"I'm fine," he muttered.

"Why don't you try it on the deck?" I suggested.

He moved the bench under the maple tree instead and stood back with a look of satisfaction on his face.

Micah looked skyward, then glanced at me and meowed once more.

Marcus shook his head. "What's wrong with right here? There's shade. There are no bees. The ground is level. It's perfect."

Before I could answer, a bird flew overhead and made a direct hit on the center of the bench seat.

Micah ducked her head. I bit my lip to keep from laughing and watched Marcus from the corner of my eye.

He stood silently for a long moment. Finally, he said, "You know, I think the bench would look great on the deck."

I nodded. "Good idea."

Later, once the weeding was done and the grass had been clipped around the flower beds, we sat on the deck steps with glasses of lemonade and lots of ice. Marcus seemed lost in thought.

"You weren't wrong to take a second look at Leitha's death," I said, "no matter what Johnny says, no matter what anyone says."

He put his free hand on my knee and gave it a squeeze. "Thanks. I know, but it has complicated the investigation into Mike Bishop's death."

"I'm not second-guessing you, but is there any chance his death is connected somehow to those car break-ins?"

He shook his head. "It's not." He ran a hand though his hair. "They're just kids—you know that, teenagers—and more important, they have alibis for the night Mike was killed. I'm glad that Mariah Taylor isn't hanging around with that bunch, though."

"She's a bright kid," I said, reaching for my glass, which was two steps below me between my feet.

"There are three kids involved as far as I can tell—a girl and two boys—and I feel confident that the girl is the ring leader. She's smart and articulate and she's got a bit of a chip on her shoulder. She's being raised by a single dad, and from what I could see, money is tight. We have them on the whipped cream incident and a couple of other car break-ins, but that's as far as it goes. They didn't have anything to do with Mike's death."

"Why didn't you tell that to Johnny? He thinks you're not working on the case."

He leaned sideways, kissed my neck and straightened up again. "Because it just happened and the lawyers and the prosecuting attorney are still talking, hopefully working out some kind of a deal that involves restitution and community service. Cleaning garbage out of ditches sounds pretty good this time of year. And I think right now nothing I could say is going to make a difference to Johnny."

"It would be such an easy solution if you found out that Mike had been killed just by some random thief."

"I don't think this case is going to be that easy," he said.

I leaned my head against his shoulder. Neither did I.

Marcus kissed the top of my head. "Could you make a list of everyone you remember being at the library for Mary's talk? I should have asked for that sooner."

"I can do that, but there's no way I'll remember everyone."

"I know," he said. "But it's a place to start."

We sat there for a little while longer, talking about the backyard and whether or not it need another raised bed. Finally

Marcus stretched and got to his feet. "Do you want to try those veggie burgers Maggie recommended?"

I looked at Micah, who wrinkled her nose. "No," I said.

"Let me rephrase." He gave me an over-the-top smile that made me think of SpongeBob SquarePants for some reason. "Hey! Let's try those veggie burgers Maggie recommended!"

"Merow!" Micah said. Rephrasing had not changed her opinion.

I laughed. "I'm willing to try them, but if they taste terrible, you have to promise we can order pizza."

"Deal," he said. "And Maggie said they're good."

I stood up and kissed the side of his mouth. "Maggie thinks herbal tea is better than coffee. I love her, but she's not a reliable source of information on this kind of thing."

The veggie burgers were actually good. Even Micah tried a tiny bite and seemed to like them. After supper I pulled up some paint swatches on my phone and we tried to decide what color to paint the bench with Micah weighing in with her opinion from time to time. Later on, we drove out to The Brick to listen to a new band. We didn't talk about Mike or Leitha and I tried not to think about them, either.

Marcus and I went out to feed the cats at Wisteria Hill the next morning.

"Do you know if Leitha shopped online?" I asked as we

drove up the hill. I was thinking out loud as much as I was talking to him.

He shot me a quick glance. "Where did that come from?"

"I'm just trying to work out a couple of things. Did she shop online?"

He kept his eyes on the road but gave his head a little shake. "Lots of people in their nineties have embraced technology, but Leitha Anderson was not one of them. No computer. No tablet. No smartphone. What is it exactly that you're trying to work out?"

"How she ended up with potassium chloride in her system. What if she took too much by mistake?" I held up a hand before he could say anything. "Just hear me out. Leitha was stubborn and opinionated. Maybe she thought it would benefit her somehow. Potassium does help the heart and the kidneys work properly, among other things, although as far as I know, most people get enough from what they eat."

"I don't disagree with your reasoning," Marcus said. "But we're still left with the same question. How did she get it? She didn't order anything online. She didn't buy it in town. There was no potassium chloride in her house. No charges for it on her credit card. And before you suggest she bought it in Minneapolis, when she went there, Jonas Quinn always drove her. She'd have had no opportunity to buy anything he wouldn't have seen."

"Maybe she stole it," I said.

"You mean, from the hospital?"

I nodded.

He shook his head. "I had the same thought. Again, no opportunity."

I sighed softly.

"Kathleen, your own timeline puts Leitha at the library for close to two hours. The medical examiner says the potassium chloride had to have been ingested there. There's not a lot of wiggle room in that. All she had in her stomach was the partly digested cookie and tea with milk and sugar."

"Did she take any pills?" I knew I was reaching.

"She took a multivitamin every day. It was a large yellow pill, not a capsule, which could have been tampered with a lot more easily. I don't see how it could have been the source of the potassium chloride."

I rubbed the back of my head with one hand. This whole thing gave me a headache. "What about blood pressure medication or something to manage her blood sugar or thyroid?"

Marcus shook his head. "There was nothing like that. The woman was as healthy as a horse. That's why she was part of that study."

"I remember that when the accident happened you didn't find any evidence that Leitha's car had been tampered with," I said. "That hasn't changed?"

He turned his head to look at me for a moment. "No, it hasn't. Leitha's death was not an accident, Kathleen. I wish it was. But it wasn't. Why are you having such a hard time with that?"

There was a knot in my stomach. "Because if someone deliberately killed Leitha, then maybe that same person also killed Mike. Maybe . . . maybe it wasn't some random burglar who panicked." I straightened up, linked my fingers together and rested my hands on the top of my head. "I know this is more emotion than logic talking. It's just how I feel right now."

"The car was checked from top to bottom. There were no mechanical issues. In fact, Lachlan had taken the car in for service the day before Leitha died."

"Harry's looking for answers. So is Johnny. So is pretty much the entire town."

"And you're afraid they're not going to like those answers."

I sighed, dropped my arms and adjusted my seat belt. "I'm afraid they're not going to get any answers," I said.

"I'm not going to give up," Marcus said. "Are you?"

I studied his profile. I knew what that determined jut of his chin meant. I shook my head. "No."

"Then everyone will get their answers eventually."

The cats all looked healthy and they seemed to still be happy in the new home Eddie had built for them. The girls' hockey team had a training session and Marcus needed to stop in at the station, so I drove home right before lunch.

Hercules was waiting in the porch. I brought him up-to-date on what I'd learned from Marcus while I made coffee.

Since I hadn't had any at lunch, I decided it was okay to have a cup of coffee now. I was very good at rationalizing my coffee drinking.

I sat at the kitchen table with my cup, a banana muffin and two sliced tomatoes. Hercules climbed onto my lap and helped me make the list that Marcus had asked me for. When I couldn't come up with any more names, I e-mailed it to him, but I didn't shut down my laptop.

"What do we know about Leitha's daughter, Eloise?" I asked the cat.

He blinked his green eyes and gave me a blank look.

"Exactly," I said. "Really, we know nothing."

I didn't actually believe Eloise had snuck back into town twice, once to kill her mother and a second time to get rid of her cousin, but maybe there was something in her life or her background that might help me. I was grasping at straws, but right now I didn't really have anything else to hold on to.

As usual, Hercules was happy to help me see what we could find online, making occasional comments about what was on the screen and swiping at the touch pad when he wanted to check out something else.

Eloise Finnamore Anderson-Hill was a fascinating person, I learned, very different from her mother. She had two daughters adopted from Korea, Nari and Min, and ran a children's clothing company that focused on sustainable practices and provided shoes and clothing to kids in need. And she had established a scholarship in her father's name—Markham Anderson. There was only one mention of the Finnamore name in a newspaper article about the scholarship.

"I know I can't change the world," Eloise had said in an interview. "But I can work on making my small corner of it better."

Hercules and I looked at Eloise's social media and her company's website. Most people called her Ellie, I learned. She was divorced. She was a vegan. She liked to hike and camp.

"How could Leitha not have been wildly proud of her daughter?" I said to Hercules. I thought about my own mother. She was my, Sarah's and Ethan's biggest cheerleader.

He blinked his green eyes at me again. It didn't make any sense to him, either.

An errant paw took me to a photo of Eloise at her mother's funeral, which had been private. She wore a navy coat over a gray dress. Mike's hand was on her shoulder, and even at a distance, she looked profoundly sad. Other than that one time, I couldn't recall ever seeing the woman in town.

There was a knock at the door.

Hercules looked expectantly at me. "Are you going to get that or should I?" I asked.

His tail flicked through the air and he made a huffy sound, his way of telling me I wasn't as funny as I thought I was.

Keith King was standing at my back door. He was about average height, strong and wiry with dark hair and dark eyes behind a pair of black stainless steel–framed glasses.

"Hi, Keith," I said. I was surprised to see him.

He smiled. "Hi, Kathleen. I'm sorry to bother you at home, but I'm going out of town for a couple of days and I didn't just want to leave this." He was holding a green file folder and he offered it to me.

"What is this?" I asked. Keith was on the library board. Was there a meeting I'd forgotten about?

"I found some papers in a book that I borrowed from the library. They look like they belong to someone tracing their family tree. You know I'm doing some of that myself. I didn't get a chance to look at the book before now, so that's why I didn't find them sooner."

"Thanks for dropping them off," I said. "Maybe I can figure out who they belong to."

"That's what I was hoping," Keith said. "There are several pages of notes in there, which means a lot of research someone will have to do again." He smiled. "We're going to see Taylor."

Keith's daughter had a summer job in St. Paul.

"Tell her we miss her at tai chi."

"I will," he said. "She's going to be home for a few days at the end of the month. I know she'll want to see you."

"We all want to see her, too."

I thanked Keith again and he left.

I took the file of papers into the kitchen. Hercules was sitting on my chair, washing his face. I pushed the laptop aside and laid the folder on the table. Hercules abandoned his beauty routine and stood up on his back legs, one white-tipped paw on the edge of the table, craning his neck for a look.

I picked up the top sheet of paper and right away I knew who had made the notes. I recognized Mike's cramped, angular handwriting. I'd seen it many times. I flipped though the pages. Some were just copies of documents with notes in the margins. Others were paragraphs of information and one page was covered with what looked like several Punnett squares. It looked as though Mike had been trying to figure out someone's eye color. Maybe he'd been trying to eliminate someone from the family tree. I remembered him telling me that back in the 1800s, the Finnamores had been a randy lot.

"I should get these to Jonas," I said to Hercules.

He yawned and jumped down to the floor. It seemed the eye color of errant Finnamores didn't interest him.

I looked up Jonas's address. There was a flea market close to where he lived that would be wrapping up in about an hour. I was searching for some old maps for a display I had planned at the library, but so far I hadn't found anything that would work. I could swing by the flea market and then drop Mike's notes off to Jonas if he was around.

I called Jonas, crossing my fingers that he was home. He was. I explained about Keith finding the papers and bringing them to me. "I'm heading to the flea market. I can drop them off afterward. I won't be that long."

"I appreciate that," Jonas said. "Do you know how to find me?"

"I do," I said.

"Then I'll see you soon."

I grabbed my bag and the folder and stepped into my canvas shoes. "I'm leaving," I called.

There was silence and then an answering meow from upstairs. I locked the back door, walked around the house to the truck and climbed inside, setting Mike's notes on the seat beside me. Out of nowhere Owen appeared on the hood of the truck. "Merow," he said, cocking his head to one side.

I knew what he wanted. Owen loved going out in the truck, but there was no way taking him with me was a good idea. I knew what would happen. Owen would do his disappearing act and then go on a self-directed tour of Jonas's house as I tried to nonchalantly swing my arms around and make contact with him while at the same time making casual conversation with Jonas.

I shook my head. "Not this time."

He got a sulky look on his face and disappeared.

I jumped out of the truck, leaving the driver's door open, felt around on the hood and somehow managed to grab him. He reappeared, looking even more disgruntled than he had before.

"Not this time," I repeated.

I set him on the path. He refused to look at me, starting around the house in a snit. He flicked his tail in my direction just as he turned the corner and then once again he disappeared.

I got back in the truck, wondering what it was like to have normal cats.

The flea market was winding down, so there weren't many people around. I didn't unearth any maps, but I did come across a poster of a large tree covered with dollar bills that would be good for Money Week in the fall.

I found Jonas's house without any difficulty. It was a beautiful Victorian, larger than I had expected, painted a creamy white with dark gray accents. It was set back from the road and the grounds looked like a park with a well-trimmed lawn, beautiful flower beds and what might have been an English-style cottage garden at the back.

Lachlan was sitting on the front steps, bent over his phone, as I pulled up. He was dressed all in black: jeans, T-shirt, high-tops. When I got out of the truck, he got to his feet and came over to me.

"Could I talk to you for a minute first before you go inside?" he asked.

"Of course," I said.

"Uncle Mike said you were really good at research and I was wondering if you could teach me how to find some information about . . . something?" He shifted awkwardly from one foot to the other.

I pushed my sunglasses up onto the top of my head. "I could try. Can you give me an idea of what the something is?"

He looked over his shoulder at the house. Whatever it was, he didn't want Jonas to know. "There's this building in Red Wing that my family owns. My Aunt Leitha was selling it to someone but I want to cancel the deal and sell it to someone else instead. She was wrong and I need to correct her mistake."

"You mean, the building that may have been the first music school in the state?" I said. "You want to sell it to Johnny?"

He looked surprised but he nodded. "He told me to just let it be, but I can't do that. If I can find proof that it was the first music school, then maybe I can stop it from being turned into a parking lot."

"You're welcome to come to the library anytime and any of us would be happy to help you, but I happen to know there are other people researching that same building, so you might want to wait a bit."

"It's Johnny, isn't it?" he said.

"I'm just going to go with 'no comment' for now," I said.

He nodded. "Okay, I can wait for a while but not forever. I can't let that building be torn down."

"How about if I happen to come across anything that might help you, I put it aside and let you know?"

He smiled. "Thank you."

Jonas came around the side of the house then. "Kathleen, hello. You found us without any difficulty?" he said.

"I did. I've driven by several times but I never realized this beautiful house was here."

"This is the Quinn family homestead. Colin—Lachlan's dad—and I grew up here. So did our father."

Lachlan pointed to a large elm tree on the other side of the driveway. "Don't get him started on all the members of the Quinn family who have fallen out of that tree," he said. "I think it's some kind of weird family tradition by now." He darted a look at Jonas and I saw the same mischievous gleam in his eye that I'd seen more than once in Mike's.

"Don't you have a couple of books left on your summer reading list that you should be pretending to read?" Jonas asked.

"Yeah, probably," Lachlan said. He looked at me. "I might come in some time and try to finish the family tree Uncle Mike was working on."

"Anytime," I said. "You might get lucky and Mary might have cookies."

He headed for the house. As he passed his uncle, Jonas put a hand on the boy's shoulder for a brief moment.

I held out the folder of papers. Jonas took them but didn't bother looking inside. "Thank you," he said. He raised an eyebrow. "Do you have time for a cup of coffee?"

"I'd like that," I said.

We walked around the side of the house, and the backyard stopped me in my tracks. "Oh, this is beautiful," I said.

The thick green lawn was bordered by curving flower beds that were bursting with color. I recognized wild roses, black-eyed Susans and lilies with colors running the gamut from pale yellow to a purple so dark, it was almost black. There were daisies, astilbes and other plants I didn't know the names of.

Jonas smiled. "Thank you. My mother, Mary-Margaret, designed the garden. When Ainsley, Lachlan's mother, was alive, they lived in this house and she took care of it. Since then I've mostly been just trying to keep all the plants alive. Thankfully, I've had a lot of help from Harry Taylor."

He gestured to a small wrought iron table sitting on a flagstone patio at the back of the house. "Please have a seat." There were three wicker chairs spaced around the table with fat flowered seat cushions, and on top sat a round wooden tray with an insulated carafe, a heavy white stoneware mug, spoons, sugar and cream. Another mug sat in front of one of the chairs.

Jonas set the file of papers on the seat of the empty chair and then poured a cup of coffee for me. I added cream and sugar to mine and took a sip.

"This is good," I said. The coffee was strong and rich, just the way I liked it.

He took a sip from his own cup and smiled. "I confess I'd choose a cup of coffee over tea or pretty much anything else. I generally only have tea if it's late in the day. I had a feeling we might be kindred souls on that front."

I smiled back at him. "Guilty," I said.

"I know I'm going to sound like an overprotective parental figure, but Lachlan asked you to help him try to document the history of that building in Red Wing that Leitha was in the process of selling, didn't he?"

I hesitated. "Yes," I finally said. "Is that a problem?"

He shook his head. "Not for me. It's something for him to focus on and right now I think it's good for him."

"I'll do a little digging on Monday and see what I can find."

"I appreciate that," Jonas said. "He's a tough kid, but he's had more loss than most adults ever have to face. We're lucky to have people like Johnny and Harry around us. They've become family."

"'Families are like pieces of art,'" I said. "'You can make them from almost anything.' Mitch Albom."

Jonas nodded. "Smart man."

Out of the corner of my eye, I saw movement. I glanced sideways as the file folder on the chair between us opened. There was no breeze but I was pretty sure there *was* a small gray tabby cat sitting on the chair. Owen had gotten in the truck after all. Somehow he had darted back and jumped inside, probably because I'd left the driver's door open when I'd gotten out to lift him off the hood. He was faster than I'd realized and for once he hadn't given himself away on the drive out or at the flea market. The little furball was getting sneakier. Had he gotten out of the truck at the flea market? I didn't want to think about that.

What I needed to do was distract Jonas so he didn't see the piece of paper that was now seemingly levitating above the flowered seat all by itself.

I set my mug on the table. "Would you mind if I took a closer look at the flower beds?" I asked.

"Of course not," Jonas said. He set his cup next to mine and got to his feet. I stood up as well and we walked over to the closest bed.

Looking at the paint box of colors, I wished I had more of a green thumb. I pointed at the plant closest to me. "I would say that's a black-eyed Susan with purple petals but I'm thinking I'd be wrong."

He smiled. "Those are *Echinacea purpurea*, purple coneflowers. They attract bees and butterflies and they're easy to grow."

I smiled. "My kind of plant." Behind us the piece of paper was moving, seemingly of its own volition, across the grass. I fervently hoped it and Owen were headed in the direction of my truck.

Jonas and I spent about ten minutes walking around, looking at the various plants. "You're welcome to come out again for another look anytime you'd like," he said. "And if you describe pretty much any of these plants to Harry, he'll know what they are."

"Thank you for the tour of the garden," I said as we walked back to the truck. I had no idea where Owen was or what he'd done with that piece of paper. "When I get to the library on Monday, I'm going to be looking for some gardening books."

"Thank you for bringing out those papers," Jonas said. "And thanks for offering to help Lachlan."

I opened the driver's door, hoping Owen was close by and would hop in. I felt something move across my foot and looked down to see my shoelace was untied. I set my bag by my feet and bent down to fasten it and just under the edge of the truck spotted the piece of paper Owen had swiped.

I didn't want to leave it there covered in cat drool and I

didn't want Jonas to see me pick it up. Luckily he was checking out the truck and I managed to pick up my bag and the paper and set them on the front seat in one more or less smooth motion.

"Kathleen, where did you get this truck?" he asked. There was something in his expression I couldn't quite read, an almost wistfulness.

"Harrison Taylor gave it to me. It's old, but it'll push through a fair amount of snow and pretty much anything else that gets in its way."

"Colin, my brother, had one just like it. It brings back a lot of good memories." He laid his hand on the front fender for a moment and I thought how Lachlan wasn't the only one who had lost way more than was fair.

I drove away with my fingers crossed that I had a furry—and invisible—stowaway. Once I was down the road beyond the Quinn driveway, I pulled over to the side of the road.

"Show yourself, Owen," I said.

Nothing.

"Right now. I'm not kidding."

Still nothing.

Was I wrong? Was he still out prowling around Jonas's yard? How on earth would I explain that I had left my cat behind?

And then I felt the tiniest brush of something against my right arm. It felt like a piece of dandelion fluff grazing my skin. Or a cat's tail. I stretched both arms over my head and then shifted sideways and brought my right hand down onto the seat. I had timed it perfectly. I had a handful of invisible cat.

Owen winked into sight and there was something cocky about the look he gave me.

"You're in so much trouble," I said, glaring at him. "Jonas almost saw you and you stole one of those pieces of paper."

He peered at the seat, spotted the piece of paper in question and set one paw on it, looking at me as though he was expecting some kind of praise. As usual, he wasn't sorry. I reached over and picked the paper up, wondering what it was that had attracted the cat's attention.

The paper was half of a page from a lined yellow notepad. I'd seen Mike making notes on a similar pad at the library and it was his writing filling the lines.

There were two Punnett squares drawn on the page. Like the notes I'd glanced at earlier, it seemed as though Mike had been trying to work out eye-color probabilities. His handwriting was hard to read. "Leitha" with a question mark was written just above the tear line. What had Mike been trying to figure out and why was Leitha's name written on the page? I had no idea.

Once again, none of this made sense.

chapter 16

Owen sat next to me all the way home, eyes fixed on the road.

"You're in trouble," I said.

"Mrr," he said.

We both knew I was wasting my breath. First of all, how did you punish a cat with klepto tendencies and the ability to disappear whenever he felt like it? It's not as though I could put him in a time-out or take away his cell phone. I couldn't even take away his supply of catnip chickens because they were stashed all over the house in hiding places I hadn't discovered yet.

I glanced over at him again. He definitely looked cocky.

I spent a good chunk of the evening trying to figure out the Punnett squares that Mike had drawn. It had been a long time since I'd had a biology class, but I remembered more than I'd expected about genetics and I found a couple of texts in the library's online catalogue.

"'A Punnett square is used to predict which traits offspring will have based on the traits of the parent,'" I read to Owen. "'It's a visual representation of the principle—put forth by Gregor Mendel by the way—that certain traits are dominant over others. It's not infallible because there can be other factors at work, but the results are a lot better than just making a wild guess.'"

Working out eye color wasn't as simple as we'd once thought it was. At one time geneticists had believed it was controlled by a single gene, which meant, for instance, that blue-eyed parents could never have a brown-eyed child.

"Except they can," I told the cat. "It's rare, but it does happen. The idea of just one gene controlling eye color was too simplistic." I remembered my professor explaining that eye color is an example of a polygenic trait. In other words, it's controlled by several different genes.

Owen wasn't the slightest bit interested in genetics. "Did you know that cats with white in their fur are believed to have a mutant gene?" I asked him as he washed his face.

Hercules had just walked into the kitchen and Owen immediately turned to look at him with an inquiring murp.

"Yes, like your brother. And you."

Hercules gave me a blank look as though he was wondering what he'd just missed. Or not.

Owen disappeared and a moment later the basement door opened a little wider.

I turned back to the computer. Maybe if I could find out what color Leitha's eyes were, I could sort out what Mike had been doing.

All of a sudden I had a lap of cat.

"Hello," I said to Hercules. "Would you like to help?"

"Mrr," he said, shifting around on my legs. Finally he was settled, eyes fixed on the screen, one paw next to the touch pad. I sometimes got the weird feeling that when I wasn't home Hercules was on the computer watching Netflix. He pretty much had the skills for it.

It took some digging, but I finally managed to find two photos of Leitha that were close enough for me to see her eyes.

"They were green," I said. I was remembering correctly.

Hercules murped his agreement. It took more poking around but I managed to learn that Leitha's mother had blue eyes. I couldn't find any photos or any references to the color of John Finnamore Senior's eyes.

I looked at the tables Mike had drawn. There were a couple of reference sources I could check at the library in the morning.

I shut off the laptop. What had he been trying to work out? And did it even have any connection to his and Leitha's deaths?

Maybe this was just a waste of time. I slumped in my chair and stared up at the ceiling. There weren't any answers up there, either.

It was busy at the library in the morning. A couple of teachers came in to look around our reference section and get a jump on planning for fall assignments. Two boxes of new books were delivered, and Patricia Queen sent me a detailed plan for the proposed quilting workshops. I pulled one genetics reference, hoping I'd have a chance to look at it during my lunch break. Then I moved over to the local-history section. I was hoping to find an article about some event that John Finnamore Senior had attended. Many of them were written with a lot of extraneous detail, like the style of shoe a man had been wearing, the cut of his suit or the color of his eyes.

"Looking for something?" Susan asked as she came around the shelving unit. I was twisted sideways, reading the call numbers on the spines of the books.

I straightened up. My left shoulder had kinked and I rubbed it with my other hand. "We have a book about the so-called upper echelon of Mayville Heights' society in the late 1800s. I can't find it."

"I think I saw it on one of the carts," she said. Today there was one thin knitting needle and one black lacquered chopstick stuck in her hair. "Do you want me to set it aside for you?"

"Please," I said.

"Are you finishing Mike's research for his family?"

"Just trying to tie up a couple of loose ends." That was true as far as it went.

"It's quiet right now," Susan said, pushing a collection of bracelets up her arm. "I could look something up if that would help."

I hesitated. "All right. I'm looking for some reference to John Finnamore Senior's eye color. I remember Mike saying he usually went by Jack."

I waited for her to ask me why I wanted that information. She just smiled and said, "No problem. I'll let you know if I find anything."

"And will you keep an eye out for any notes Mike might have left behind. Keith King found some papers that belonged to Mike in a book Keith had borrowed. I just want to make sure we haven't missed anything else."

"Will do," Susan said.

Roma came by midmorning with four large zucchini. She handed them to me. "This is partly a thank-you for feeding the cats and partly a 'please take these' because I have so many."

"You're welcome," I said. "I'm thinking chocolate zucchini bread sounds good."

She smiled. "I'm thinking I need to bring you more zucchini."

"Rebecca would probably take some. She makes a wonderful vegetarian lasagna."

"I'll call her," Roma said. "Or maybe I'll just leave a bag on the front step, ring the doorbell and run."

I laughed. "It can't be that bad."

"Oh, but it is. They're taking over my garden. I get up in the morning and I swear there are twice as many of the things as there were the night before." She looked around. "Is Mary here?" she asked.

"She is," I said. "She's putting out new magazines. Do you have zucchini for her as well?"

Roma smoothed a hand over her dark hair, tucking it behind one ear. "No. I need to talk to her. After I had lunch with you and Maggie, I called Sandra to talk more about doing another burlesque show. It looks like the shelter is going to need a new heating system."

I made a face. "That's not good."

"The reality is that they need a new building, which means a major fund-raising push. I asked Sandra if she would talk to whoever Zorro was and see if he'd do another show as a way of launching a fund-raiser for a new home for the shelter. She refused."

"Did she say why?" I asked. Working with Sandra on the library board, I'd found her to be a very reasonable, easy-to-get-along-with person.

Roma shook her head. "That's the thing. All she said was no and that Zorro's performance was a onetime thing. There's no point in putting on the show without him, not if we want to generate a lot of attention for the fund-raising campaign, but Sandra won't budge. I want to try to appeal to the person myself if Mary will tell me who he is. Sandra wouldn't. It's not just the heating system. When they were working on the roof, they uncovered some structural problems with the building. The shelter can probably get through this winter but beyond that they need a new home. As it is they're going to have to close one room, which means they're going to have to turn animals away."

"C'mon," I said. "I'll walk you over to her."

Mary listened to what Roma had to say but she wouldn't budge.

"I'm sorry," she said. "I'll help you in any way I can, but as far as Zorro is concerned, that was something that isn't going to be repeated."

"If I could just talk to him," Roma said.

Mary just shook her head. "I'm sorry."

I walked Roma back to the front entrance. "I really thought she'd tell me who he is," she said. "I don't understand why they're both being so secretive."

"I can't promise anything," I said, "but give me some time. I'll talk to Mary again."

Roma hugged me. "Thanks, Kath," she said.

I stood outside on the steps, trying to figure out who had played Zorro and why, after dancing onstage bare chested in a cape and tights, he did not want anyone to know who he was.

I tried to think of who would bring out such unequivocal loyalty from both Sandra and Mary. The two most likely candidates were Everett and Burtis, and from what I'd seen of Zorro's performance, it wasn't either of them.

When I went back inside, Susan waved me over to the desk. "Blue," she said with a smile.

"I thought we settled on gray," I said. It had taken a month for us to come to a consensus on a paint color for the walls of the staff room, and now she was changing her vote?

She frowned at me for a moment and then the frown cleared. "I'm not talking about the staff room. I'm talking about John Finnamore. His eyes were blue. Light blue by all accounts. I read three of them."

"Thank you," I said.

She smiled again. "You're welcome. I hope it helps."

I nodded. "So do I."

I went up to my office. There was a slim chance that Leitha's blue-eyed parents could have had a green-eyed child. So what had Mike been trying to work out? Once again it seemed I was left with nothing but a handful of straw.

When I went back downstairs about an hour later, I spotted Mary shelving in the children's department. I walked over to her.

"I know what you want and you're wasting your time," she said without preamble as she straightened a row of picture books. "If it were possible to help Roma, believe me, I would, but it's not."

"Could you at least ask Zorro if he'd talk to Roma?" I said.

She looked at me. "Do you think I like the idea of cats being put down because there's no shelter for them to go to?"

"I know you don't," I said.

Mary might have been able to take someone down with just one well-placed kick, but she was very much a mushball inside.

"Then take me at my word when I tell you that there is no way Zorro will ride again and you just need to accept it."

Lachlan showed up around two o'clock. He was dressed all in black again. "If it's okay, I thought maybe I would see what I can find about the old music school in Red Wing after all. I mean, I wasn't doing anything else."

"Of course it's okay," I said. "I'm thinking the best place to start would be with the newspaper. The only problem is, the older issues haven't been digitized, so you'll have to use the microfilm reader."

"Okay," he said with a shrug.

I got him set up at the machine and showed him how to scroll through the pages. "Try looking for references to the school in articles and photographs but keep an eye out for any ads for classes or recitals."

He nodded. "I can do that."

"If you have any problems, I'm around and Susan is at the desk."

I left him to it, thinking how much he reminded me of

Mike, who had also spent some time going through back issues of newspapers. It wasn't that they looked alike, but Lachlan seemed to be capable of the same level of concentration and the ability to tune out everything else that Mike had had. Right now Lachlan was leaning forward, watching the screen, just the way Mike had, his eyebrows drawn together in a frown in exactly the same fashion.

I was in the staff room about half an hour later getting a cup of coffee before I started to work on the staff schedule when Harry appeared in the doorway.

"Hi," he said. "Susan said you were up here."

"I'm getting fortified for some paperwork," I said, holding up the pot. "Would you like a cup?"

He shook his head. "No, thanks. I just wanted to let you know that I talked to Ritchie and he wasn't spending Wednesday nights with Mike."

"Thanks," I said. "It was a bit of a long shot."

"Do you really think it's important?" Harry asked. "Maybe Mike was seeing someone and just wanted to keep it to himself."

I leaned back against the counter and folded my hands around my cup. "You're probably right."

"I have faith in you, Kathleen," Harry said. "I know you can figure out what happened." He gestured toward the back of the building. "I'll be out at the gazebo if you need me."

Instead of going back to my office, I stayed where I was, leaning against the counter. Harry had faith in me but I wasn't so sure that I had faith in myself.

Mike had probably just been seeing someone that he wasn't ready to introduce to his family and friends. And he'd likely been killed by some random prowler. It happened, even in a place as small and safe as Mayville Heights. My problem was the fact that I couldn't shake the feeling that that *wasn't* what had happened. I didn't know why I felt that way. I just had some feeling, some instinct that there was more to Mike Bishop's death than it seemed on the surface. I thought about what Harrison had said to me, "Just rely on your instincts and everything will be just fine."

I was probably tilting at windmills à la Don Quixote but I wasn't going to give up on figuring out where Mike had been on Wednesday nights for the past couple of months.

I did some work on the schedule and then went downstairs to give Susan a break at the front desk.

"It's been quiet so far," she said. "Did Harry find you?"

"He did," I said. "Thanks for sending him up."

"Lachlan Quinn is still on the microfilm reader and the monitor on the second computer is acting up again. I did your 'whack it on the side' thing and it seems to be okay for now."

"The board meeting's this week. After that, I should be able to order the new computers." I held up my crossed fingers.

"I can't wait," Susan said. "I may make a bonfire out of the old ones and dance naked around it in the moonlight."

"I'm pretty sure you can't burn computers," I said. "They release toxic chemicals into the air."

"Okay, so naked dancing in the moonlight it is." She grinned.

"Or we could just have cake."

She thought about it for a moment. "Yeah, or we could just have cake." She stretched and yawned. "Please tell me there's coffee."

I smiled. "I made a new pot."

Susan smiled back at me. "I knew there was a reason I like you."

There were three books sitting on the counter. She put a hand on top of them and her smile faded. "Mike requested those," she said.

It wasn't the first time books had come in for someone who had died. That little bit of unfinished business always left me feeling sad, even if I hadn't known the person beyond what they had liked to read.

The top book on the stack was about the *Mayflower*, the second one was about life in England in the early 1600s and the last was *The Genetics of Eye Color*.

"I'll send them back," I said. "Go take your break."

She headed for the stairs and I picked up the books. I had suggested the one about the *Mayflower* and another source had mentioned the book about life in seventeenth-century England. The genetics text had to have something to do with those Punnett squares.

Holding the book in my hands, I had a crazy thought that

maybe Mike had gotten the idea that Leitha wasn't a Fin-namore because of something he had learned during his re-search. I thought about the picture he had shown me of Leitha with her parents. Leitha didn't look a lot like them but that might have been her stern appearance in the photograph. Was it possible? And if bizarrely it was true, then did that have any-thing to do with either of their deaths?

chapter 17

I spent the rest of the afternoon with questions about what Mike had been trying to work out turning over in my head. If she'd been faced with proof that she wasn't a Finnamore, what would Leitha have done? It had been such a huge part of her identity. If—and that was a very big if—Mike had found some reason to suspect she hadn't been part of the Finnamore legacy, I didn't see her just accepting that. She would have needed more solid proof than just his suspicions. And the color of her eyes proved nothing with respect to whether or not she was biologically part of that family.

Mike was smart enough not to just rely on eye color to prove something like that. Maybe I needed to look at another

Finnamore family trait that was more genetically straightfor-ward. I was probably tilting at windmills again. I rubbed both temples. I had a headache again.

Lachlan had found some information about the music school in the newspaper. "I'm on the right track," he said to me. "I know it. Thanks for suggesting the newspaper and showing me how to look at it. I'll be back to see what else I can find."

I was happy to see him smile.

"Do you know where Levi is?" I said to Susan. "I need some help carrying in some boxes."

"He's scraping gum off the bottom of one of the tables in the children's section," she said. "What is it with people and gum in the library? Don't they know what garbage cans are for?"

"I don't know," I said.

Gum stuck all sorts of odd places in the building was a chronic problem for us.

"Would it be okay if I made some signs?" Susan asked. "Just something that says, 'Please put your gum in the garbage can,' or something like that?"

"It's fine with me." I wasn't sure signs would make a differ-ence but it wouldn't hurt to try.

Levi was on his hands and knees under one of the big round tables in the children's department, scraping at the underside with the plastic scraper. His mind was clearly somewhere else because, when I called his name, he started and banged his head on the table.

"I'm sorry," I said as he backed out from underneath. "I didn't mean to scare you. I just need some help carrying some boxes up to the workroom."

"It's not your fault," he said. "That's the second time I've done that in the last ten minutes. My brain can't seem to remember there's a table just four inches above my head." He held one hand just above his hair and moved it through the air.

Levi looked tired. He'd missed a patch on his left jawline when he'd shaved and he wasn't quite looking me in the eye.

"What's wrong?" I asked.

"I'm okay," he replied just a little too quickly.

I could easily think of half a dozen things that could have been wrong in the life of someone his age. I hoped it was one of the minor ones.

"I didn't ask if you were okay. I asked what's wrong." I waited.

He didn't seem to quite know what to do with his hands. He ran them back through his hair, then tugged at the front of his shirt.

"I don't want to get anyone in trouble."

"Are you trying to convince someone to break the law or hurt themselves or another person?"

"No," he said. "I would never do anything like that."

"Then you're not going to get anyone in trouble. They

might get themselves in trouble but that's on them, not on you." My mother had used that logic on me many times. Some of them it had actually worked.

"Mrs. Anderson, the woman who died in that car accident a few months ago—is it true what I heard? That is wasn't an accident."

I nodded. "It looks that way." My stomach suddenly felt like I was on a roller coaster.

"She was going home from here," Levi continued, "after Mary's talk, right?"

"That's right." I wanted to push him to get to the point, but I was afraid if I did, he'd stop talking altogether.

He rubbed his hands on his black jeans. "That day, I heard Mrs. Anderson arguing with someone. She was really angry."

"Do you know who she was arguing with?"

He nodded. "Yeah. And the thing is, I just know that . . . that he wouldn't have killed her."

"So then you can't get that person in trouble."

He looked doubtful.

"Levi, who was it?" I asked. I had a feeling I knew the answer.

He looked down at his feet. "Johnny Rock."

That was what I had expected him to say. "I know they argued. Johnny told me."

Levi still looked troubled. "Did he tell you what he said to her?"

"He told me they'd had words over a business deal."

He couldn't seem to keep his hands still. He ran a hand over his head. He pulled at a loose thread on his shirt. "He wouldn't have killed an old lady. I don't want him to be in trouble because of what I heard."

"Levi, is this something the police need to hear?" I asked.

He looked down at his feet. "I don't know. Maybe. It's just that Johnny said something they might take the wrong way."

I slowly let out a breath. "I don't think Johnny could kill anyone, either—old or not. So what did he say? 'I wish you were dead'?" I smiled. "I'll tell you a little secret. When I was not much younger than you are, I said that to my mother more than once when I was fighting with her. But I didn't mean it and no one really thought I did."

Levi almost smiled. "I can't picture you as a teenager," he said.

"Sometime, I'll show you some slightly embarrassing photos from back then," I said.

He scuffed one foot on the floor. "Okay. Johnny didn't exactly say he wished she was dead but it was pretty close. He said, 'When you're dead, I will dance on your grave, old woman, and it can't come soon enough for me.'"

Given how angry I knew Johnny had been at the time, the words didn't surprise me. It also didn't surprise me that he hadn't volunteered that he'd said them.

"So do I need to talk to the police?" Levi asked.

"How about I tell Detective Gordon what you just told me, and if he needs to talk to you, he'll let you know."

His shoulders sagged with relief. "Thanks, Kathleen," he said. "I'll go get those boxes for you."

Once the cartons of books were upstairs, I called Marcus and explained what Levi had told me. "I don't think it's a big deal," I said. "But I thought I should let you know."

"Thanks," he said. "Johnny's feelings about Leitha are pretty clear. I don't need to talk to Levi."

"For the record, I don't think Johnny killed Leitha no matter what he said to her, and I'm certain he didn't kill Mike."

I pictured Marcus probably shaking his head at the phone. "For the record, right now I'm just going to say, 'no comment.'"

Marcus showed up just after we'd closed the library. I was about to get in the truck and Harry was sweeping the back end of the parking lot. The Reading Club kids had taken some vegetables home, and there were dirt and the odd radish all over the pavement.

I waited by the truck as Marcus walked over to me. He raised one hand in hello to Harry. "Kathleen, did you by any chance talk to Johnny this afternoon?" he asked.

"If you mean, did I call and warn him that Levi had heard him telling Leitha how happy he'd be when she was dead? No."

He had the good sense to look a little embarrassed. "I'm sorry," he said. "I didn't mean to accuse you of anything. I just wondered if he might have come in or called for any reason. You did say he made a big donation to the computer fund."

"I haven't talked to Johnny at all today. Why?"

"I need to talk to Harry," he said.

That didn't answer my question, so I followed him across the lot. He asked Harry the same question: Had he talked to Johnny this afternoon?

Harry shook his head. "I haven't talked to Johnny for a couple of days." He pulled off his hat, ran a hand over his bald head and put it back on again. "More than any of the rest of us, Johnny is struggling with Mike's death. They were close and I think Mike would have ended up going on the road with Johnny for at least part of the time, even if the rest of us didn't." He stopped and took a couple of deep breaths. "Mike was the reason we ended up getting together for the Last Bash. It was his idea and he nagged the rest of us until we were all in. The two of them had plans and I think Johnny's having a hard time letting go of them." He focused on Marcus. "No offense, but we need answers and the sooner the better."

"I know," Marcus said. "I'm trying to get you those answers. There are a couple of things I need to talk to Johnny about, but I haven't been able to find him."

"If I hear from him, I'll tell him to call you," Harry said.

Marcus nodded. "Thanks."

I said good night to Harry and walked back to the truck with Marcus. "You can't actually think Johnny killed either one of them?" I said. "He had no reason."

"My job is to gather the evidence."

I gave him a look.

He sighed. "The problem is, no one had a reason to want Mike dead as far as I can see. No one had a motive to kill Leitha, either. She was difficult, no question, but she was an annoyance, like a mosquito buzzing around your head, not a threat to anyone. I'm going to check Eric's. I'll call you later."

I watched him drive away and then I unlocked the truck, set my messenger bag on the seat and climbed inside. When I turned to head toward Mountain Road and home, I looked out over the water and the Riverwalk and it occurred to me that I might know where Johnny was. I headed in that direction instead.

As I drove, I thought about the argument Levi had over-heard between Leitha and Johnny. Those words "When you're dead, I will dance on your grave, old woman, and it can't come soon enough for me" didn't sound like a threat to me. It almost sounded like Johnny had been gloating.

I thought about Lachlan, working so hard to find some jus-tification to stop the deal for that property in Red Wing. Lach-lan had said Johnny didn't want the teen to waste his time researching the old building. That gave me an idea.

I parked in the lot where the concert stage had been set up. That night felt like such a long time ago. A man was standing by the edge of the embankment, looking out over the water, hands stuffed in his pockets.

I walked across the grass toward him. "Hey, Johnny," I said when I got close.

He turned and gave me what passed for a smile from him these days. "Hey, Kathleen. What are you doing here?"

"Looking for you."

The water was dark and angry and the clouds were low and heavy. It was going to rain soon.

"You were the new buyer for the building in Red Wing, weren't you?" I asked. "The buyer who was going to turn the property into a parking lot. You scammed Leitha. That's why you weren't worried. That's why you told Lachlan to let go of his plan to stop the sale. You didn't want to stop the sale."

He was nodding before I finished speaking. "Yeah. I bested her. You have no idea how hard it was not to rub her face in that, to keep it secret."

"I can imagine."

"It wasn't just about the building. It was the way she treated Mike and Jonas. Part of it was because I hated how she kept pressuring Lachlan about college and threatening not to let him have the Finnamore money for his education, as though studying music was somehow not good enough. I wanted her out of the kid's life but I didn't make it happen. Mike cared about the old bat, you know. And that tells you everything you need to know about him right there."

I nodded because I couldn't get any words past the lump in my throat.

"So why were you looking for me?" Johnny asked.

I cleared my throat. "Marcus needs to talk to you. I think you should tell him what you just told me."

Johnny pulled out his phone. "What's his number?"

chapter 18

I waited with Johnny until Marcus arrived.

"I would never tell you how to grieve," I said when I caught sight of Marcus pulling in next to my truck in the parking lot, "because something like that is so intensely personal, plus it annoys the crap out of me when people do that."

Johnny gave me a small smile, the first genuine one I'd seen from him in a while.

"But I am going to remind you that if Mike were standing here instead of me, he would tell you to grab life by the—" I pictured Mike onstage explaining his definition of a good friend. I smiled. "By the athletic supporter and live every second you've got because none of us knows how long that's going to be."

I put a hand on his shoulder for a moment and then headed over to meet Marcus.

"Thank you for getting Johnny to call me," he said. "I thought you were going home."

I knew that meant *Why didn't you just tell me where you thought Johnny was?* Since he hadn't asked me that directly, all I said was "I'm going home now."

I started for the truck. Marcus didn't say, *I'll call you later,* and neither did I.

After supper, once again I sat at the table with my laptop. I checked my e-mail. Susan had scanned the documents she'd found that referred to John Finnamore's eye color and e-mailed them to me. I also had an e-mail from Roma with a fairly large attachment. The subject line was THE BURLESQUE SHOW.

I opened Susan's e-mail first. Two different society-page articles mentioned John Finnamore's blue eyes and dark hair. I had the feeling I'd gotten way off on a tangent. I hadn't learned anything that put me closer to figuring out who had killed Mike.

"Does any of this really matter?" I asked Hercules, who was sitting at my feet, carefully washing his chest.

He looked up and meowed loudly and enthusiastically. He seemed to think it did. I wasn't so sure anymore.

I heard the washer shut off. I went down to the basement and discovered Owen sitting in the empty laundry basket on top of the dryer, both paws up on the end of the basket.

When Ethan and Sarah were very small, I would take the two of them sledding in a park close to where we lived. I'd stick them in our laundry basket—leaving behind a pile of dirty clothes on the floor—tie the basket to an old metal toboggan we had and then I'd jump on the back and we'd go like stink down the steepest hills there.

Ethan was always in the front of the basket, two little mittened hands holding on to the end, a huge grin on his face, with Sarah behind him with an equally big smile on her face. Dad insisted that that was the reason they both had lead feet.

The cat reminded me of Ethan. For all I knew, maybe Owen was imagining himself hurtling down a snowy hill.

I moved the wet towels into the dryer. Owen leaned his head over the side of the laundry basket and watched. "You know, if you could just learn how to set the timer, I could get you to do this and save me a trip up and down the stairs."

He looked at me and yawned. Cat for *Not happening*.

When I got back upstairs, I found Hercules standing up on my chair, looking at something on the laptop. Somehow, he'd managed to open Roma's e-mail and get into the photos from the burlesque show.

"How did you do that?" I said.

He ducked his head as though modestly trying to say, *Oh, it was nothing*.

A photo of Zorro strutting his stuff on the middle of the stage out at The Brick filled the screen. I smiled, then leaned over and closed the image. I thought of Roma's frustration with trying to organize another show. I wished there was a way to convince Mary to at least plead Roma's case to whoever Zorro was.

I scooped up Hercules, sat down and settled him on my lap. He immediately reached a paw toward the computer and Zorro filled the computer screen again.

"I don't have time for this right now," I said.

He gave an insistent meow that I knew meant he wanted me to look at the photo.

I yawned and stretched. "You're so stubborn," I said.

His whiskers twitched. A pair of green eyes was locked on my face. I glared back at him, which was a waste of time because he never lost a staring contest. Neither did Owen. "Fine," I said. "I will look at the picture."

I pulled the laptop a bit closer, centered the photo of Zorro and studied it. His fencing foil was thrust forward, his cape swirled behind him and he was giving the crowd a wicked grin as he swiveled his hips from side to side. I couldn't see what Hercules thought was so important about the image. Maybe he'd just been poking at the touch pad because it was fun. Maybe the photograph didn't matter at all.

And then I noticed something on Zorro's left hip. I used the magnifying feature to get a close look. The image was blurry but I could just make out the tops of two tiny fingers, spaced apart like they were part of some hand gesture tattooed on the man's hip.

I zoomed out again and looked at the man carefully: his

body type, his smile. And suddenly I got it. I slumped against the chair back. "Mike Bishop was Zorro," I said aloud.

Hercules had already jumped down to the floor and was washing his face. He meowed his agreement without looking up from his ablutions.

Mike was Zorro. Suddenly it all made sense. That was why both Mary and Sandra had refused to put Roma in touch with the mystery dancer. They couldn't. "Take me at my word when I tell you that there is no way Zorro will ride again," Mary had said to me. I looked at the photo one more time. It seemed so obvious now. Why hadn't it occurred to me before? Mike had the soul of a performer and a huge, kind heart. Getting up on that stage to help the no-kill shelter was exactly the kind of thing he would have done.

Hercules had stopped washing his face and was looking up at me as though he wanted something.

"Thank you for pointing out the photo," I said. "I'm sorry I didn't take you seriously at first."

And then, in case he hadn't been looking for a little vindication, I got him a couple of sardine crackers.

It was raining when I got to the library the next morning. I was unlocking the main doors and juggling my messenger bag, my coffee mug and my umbrella when Mary came up the steps and grabbed my cup just before I dropped it. I didn't have a good record with coffee mugs.

"Thank you," I said as we stepped inside.

I shut off the alarm and unlocked the second set of doors. Mary handed me my coffee. Then she flipped on the lights and pushed down the hood of her yellow slicker.

"It's not fit for man nor beast," she said, patting her hair.

I looked at her, thinking it must have been hard to keep her emotions in check when Roma and I were pressuring her to tell us Zorro's real name. She'd known Mike forever.

"I'm sorry," I said.

Mary was patting the pockets of her raincoat, looking for her keys or her phone probably. "I don't think you're responsible for this weather, Kathleen," she said without looking up.

"I didn't mean that. I mean, I'm sorry Roma and I pushed you so hard yesterday."

She did look up then. Something she saw in my expression made her shake her head. "Sometimes I think you can look right into people's heads," she said. "You figured it out, didn't you?"

"That Mike was Zorro? Yeah, I did."

"How the hell did you do that?"

I explained about the tattoos he and Johnny had gotten. "Roma sent me some photos from the show. It was really just chance that I spotted it." Chance and a small tuxedo cat, to be specific.

She laughed. "Shows how much attention I paid. I didn't even notice he had a tattoo."

We headed for the stairs. "It really was a last-minute thing, Mike getting up there as Zorro?" I said.

"Very last minute," Mary said. "We needed to get people's attention and I knew Mike was comfortable onstage."

"How did you come up with the costume?"

She laughed. "A little ingenuity and a lot of luck. The pants were his bike pants. His gym bag was in the backseat of his car. We made the mask out of one of my scarves."

I unlocked my office door and dropped my things on my desk chair, stopping to hang up my damp jacket. Mary waited in the doorway.

"What about the cape?" I asked.

"Remember I said it took a lot of luck? The cape was one of those lucky things. Sandra made it for a vampire routine and then decided the rest of the costume probably crossed a line. The hat was something we had in our costume stash and the fencing foil was another piece of luck. It came from the high school. It was used in a play they put on last year. One of the history teachers drove down and grabbed it for me. She's a cat person."

"How did you manage to keep Mike's identity a secret?"

We went down to the staff room and I started the coffee while Mary hung up her things.

"We were using the office as a dressing room, but there was a small bathroom back there as well for staff. I basically waited until no one was looking and pushed Mike inside." She made a shoving motion with one hand.

"I thought if we could keep Zorro's identity a secret that would keep people talking and keep the fund-raiser on people's minds. Mike was game." Mary pressed her lips together for a moment. "I don't think I've ever laughed so hard in my life as when I was trying to get all of his hair under that scarf. I knew if people saw those curls, the jig would be up." She looked at me. "The reason we kept the secret for so long was that Mike wanted to bring back Zorro for another fundraiser—ironically just the thing Roma wants to do. In fact, he'd been getting together with Sandra on Wednesday nights to work on a new routine."

Wednesday nights. Now I knew what Mike had been doing. Now I understood why he'd kept it a secret. I also knew that secret had had nothing to do with his death.

I glanced at Mary, who seemed lost in thought. "I don't think he'd mind you telling Roma," I said as I got the cream out of the small refrigerator.

Mary nodded. "It was such a good night. To tell the truth, I was looking forward to doing it all over again."

She swallowed a couple of times and I had to blink away the unexpected sting of tears.

"I will call Roma," Mary said, her voice suddenly hoarse. "Make sure you tell that man of yours that someone needs to be held accountable."

Despite the rain—or maybe because of it—it was a very busy day at the library. It was close to two o'clock before I got to have lunch and I got only half my sandwich eaten before Abigail came up to tell me that the door to the loading dock was leaking. I called Harry, who was able to do a temporary fix that stopped the water coming in.

"It might—*might*—be possible to order a new seal for that door," he said. "Otherwise you're going to need a new door. Water's coming in now. It's going to be a lot worse this winter." He made a face. "Let's hope this is the last bit of substandard work from Will Redfern."

Will Redfern was the original contractor for the library renovations. He and his crew had done some quality work and some that was outright shoddy. Harry and Oren Kenyon—with some help from Harry's brother, Larry, who was an electrician—had fixed most of the problems. Luckily there had been nothing major until now. A new loading dock door wasn't in the budget.

"Let me see if I can track down a door seal," Harry said. "We might get lucky."

"Fingers crossed," I said.

When I got home, I found both cats in the living room. Owen was on the chair by the phone and Hercules sat on the footstool next to the calendar Ruby had given me. It had somehow been flipped open to April and it almost seemed like they had been admiring themselves.

"Get down," I said.

Hercules looked at Owen. Owen looked at me. Neither one of them moved. I didn't have time to argue with them. I started for the stairs.

"I could have gotten some nice, well-behaved goldfish," I said. "Or a cute little hamster." We'd had this one-sided conversation before.

I looked back at them in time to see Owen exchange a look with his brother. I'm pretty sure he was rolling his eyes.

Since I'd had just part of a sandwich for lunch, I was hungry. The refrigerator and cupboards weren't quite in the realm of Old Mother Hubbard, but they were close. I found an onion, a rubbery carrot and two suspiciously soft tomatoes. I cut them all up and added half of one of the zucchini Roma had given me. I stir-fried the veggies with hot sauce and added a fried egg on top. It was filling and healthy, but I needed to get groceries soon.

It was still raining, so I drove down to tai chi and was lucky to snag a parking spot not too far away. I opened my umbrella and ran through the puddles to the studio door, where I shook the umbrella before I darted inside.

Ruby was sitting on the bench at the top of the stairs, changing her shoes.

"The calendar definitely gets two paws of approval," I said. I told her how I'd found Owen and Hercules when I got home. "I think fame is going to their heads."

Ruby smiled. "'In ancient times cats were worshipped as gods; they have not forgotten this.'"

I smiled. "Terry Pratchett."

Maggie worked us hard and I was sticky and warm by the

time we finished the whole form at the end of the class. And I was hungry again. I drove over to Eric's for something to eat, promising myself I'd make a grocery list in the morning.

I ordered a turkey sandwich to go, which I knew Eric would make with Swiss cheese, tomato, sunflower sprouts and cranberry mayo. Because it was raining, I also got a cup of coffee.

"It should be only about five minutes," Claire said.

I sat on a stool at the counter. My cell phone buzzed in my jacket pocket. I pulled it out and checked the screen. It was Roma.

"I need a favor," she said.

"Name it," I said.

"Could you and Marcus feed the Wisteria Hill cats in the morning?"

I wasn't sure about Marcus but I could. "Of course."

"I'm sorry it's such short notice. I have to go to Red Wing to assist on an emergency surgery on a police dog. Eddie's gone to Minneapolis. His plan was to drive back early in the morning and go right to the rink."

"It's not a problem," I said. "I love any chance I get to see Lucy and the other cats."

I heard her exhale with relief. "Thanks," she said. "You're a lifesaver."

I wished her good luck with the surgery, we said good-bye and I put my phone back in my pocket.

The diner was quiet. Maybe because it was raining. There

was a man standing in front of me at the counter in a dark blue slicker. It was Jonas Quinn, I realized. I touched his shoulder and he turned, smiling when he saw it was me.

"Kathleen, how are you?" he said.

"A little damp. Otherwise I'm fine. How are you?"

"I'm on my way to what I expect will be a very boring meeting. Otherwise *I'm* fine. And by the way, thanks for the help you gave Lachlan the other day."

"It was no trouble," I said. "He's a great kid."

Jonas's smile got wider. "Yes, he is."

His fingers were tapping out a rhythm on the edge of the counter and it struck me that he seemed to have the same musical bent as his nephew. Claire came out then with four take-out cups in a cardboard tray plus a paper take-out bag. She ran down the contents—three were coffees, each with a different permutation of cream and sugar, and the fourth container was tea.

"Would you like milk and sugar for the tea?" Claire asked.

"Just some milk, please," Jonas said. "The tea is mine and I don't like my drinks sweet."

She smiled. "My grandfather says the same thing. He says, 'I'm sweet enough already.'" She leaned sideways and looked at me. "Your food will be ready in just a minute, Kathleen," she said.

Jonas picked up the tray of drinks and the take-out bag. "It was good to see you, Kathleen," he said.

"You too," I said. "I hope your meeting is short and interesting."

He raised both eyebrows and smiled. "Me too."

I was restless when I got home. Marcus hadn't called, probably because he was working on one or both cases. I thought about what he'd said: "The problem is, no one had a reason to want Mike dead. . . . No one had a motive to kill Leitha, either. She was difficult, no question, but she was an annoyance . . . not a threat to anyone."

I kept coming back to those Punnett squares Mike had drawn. Even though I'd told Hercules they didn't matter, I couldn't seem to let go of the idea that somehow they did. I thought about all the times I'd seen Mike working at the library, all the times he'd waved me over. I couldn't think of a single time when he'd been drawing one of those squares.

I looked at the half sheet of yellow paper again. Something about it seemed wrong. I could think of only one occasion when I'd seen Mike with his head bent over a sheet of yellow paper. He'd mostly used wide-ruled white paper. I closed my eyes and tried to remember what I'd seen. Jonas and Lachlan had come in to take Mike to lunch. I had taken them upstairs because Mike was in our workroom. As he looked up, I remembered him jamming several pages into a book and closing the cover. Several yellow sheets of paper. I'd thought he had been marking his place but now it struck me that maybe he had been hiding them instead. But from whom? From me? From Jonas and Lachlan? I didn't know. Was I seeing something that hadn't really happened?

I found a marker and pulled a flattened cardboard box out of the recycling bin. I spread the cardboard out on the table and drew out the Finnamore family tree starting with John Finnamore Senior. Below Finnamore Senior I added his two children, Leitha and John Junior. The next generation, Eloise Anderson-Hill, Elizabeth Bishop and Mary-Margaret Quinn followed. Underneath, I wrote in Mike, Jonas and his brother, Colin, along with Eloise's daughters, Min and Nari. Lachlan had the last row to himself. I added spouses where I knew their names.

The diagram looked a little lopsided. Because there had been so many years between Leitha and her brother, Eloise was actually closer in age to Mike, Jonas and Colin—than she was to their mothers, her first cousins.

Plotting everyone's eye color was just too complicated, so I decided to try doing hair texture instead. It was simpler.

Leitha Finnamore Anderson had had curly hair. I wrote *CC* beside her name. I remembered that Susan had included a photo of Leitha and her parents when she'd sent me the information about John Senior's eye color. I got my laptop and looked at it again. Leitha's father had had curly hair. *CC* went next to his name as well.

I studied the photo carefully. Leitha's mother had had wavy hair I realized, not curly. It was a distinction some people had trouble making. That meant she had one curly-hair gene and one straight-hair gene. I put *C*s by her name. So Leitha could easily have been their child. Eloise had the same hair as her mother. Min and Nari were adopted, so they had no Finnamore DNA.

It wasn't hard to find photos of Mike's parents. They had the same curls their son did. I kept going mostly out of curiosity. Mary-Margaret Finnamore Quinn had wavy hair, not curly. Her son, Colin, had a head full of those Finnamore curls. And Jonas, who wasn't a Finnamore, had wavy hair like their father. Ainsley Quinn, Colin's wife, also had a gorgeous head full of blond curls.

I stared at my handiwork. I thought about Lachlan's unruly hair. I pictured him with his head leaning in close to the microfilm reader. "A tangle of curls," Mary had called his hair. But it wasn't really curly, I realized.

Lachlan's hair was wavy, which wasn't possible.

I got the piece of paper that Owen had swiped and looked at it again. What if Mike had been trying to work out Lachlan's eye color, not Leitha's? I thought about Jonas coming into the library that day with Lachlan. It had been just a few days before the concert. What if I was right about why Mike had stuffed those pages in the book and closed it? I looked at Owen. "What if he *was* hiding them?" I said.

I had wondered why none of the staff had checked the pages of the book in which Keith had discovered Mike's notes before Keith borrowed it. Mike had been around the library enough to know how things worked. He could have easily put the book with other ones Keith had requested. Whoever had checked Keith out could have missed those sheets of paper stuck inside the book, especially if it had been busy.

I took a sip of my coffee. There were only a couple of mouthfuls left now, and they were cold and a bit too sweet for me since some of the sugar had settled to the bottom of the cup even though Claire had stirred it well before she handed it to me.

I tapped the marker on the table. "Leitha was adamant about the importance of the family line," I said, "and she thought telling the truth was more important than discretion or hurt feelings." I remembered hearing her tell Mary the day that they had argued, with a great deal of pride in her voice, that the Finnamores could trace their family tree, unsullied, back to the *Mayflower*. Jonas had said that family was more than biology. Leitha had snorted and said of course *he* would say that.

I thought about my own family and the similarities between Ethan, Sarah and me, how Ethan made me think of Mom in so many ways. They were both born performers.

I thought about Lachlan's wavy hair, his green eyes and his gentle manner so different from the more outgoing Finnamores, so much like soft-spoken Jonas.

"Lachlan is Jonas Quinn's son," I said. It was the only explanation that made sense.

Behind me a voice said, "Yes, he is."

chapter 19

I turned around slowly. Jonas was standing in the kitchen doorway, pointing a gun at me.

"You're very smart. I knew you'd figure it all out," he said. "I wish you hadn't, though."

I swallowed against the sour taste in the back of my throat and tried not to panic. Owen leaned around the side of the chair and stared with curiosity at Jonas.

"Mike figured it out, too," I said.

"Not at first." Except for the gun, Jonas seemed just like the man who had come into the library, who had shown me around his garden, who had laughed with us all at Eric's.

"Leitha figured it out first."

He nodded. "She never let me forget that my mother was really my stepmother and I wasn't a real Finnamore."

"And she was going to tell Lachlan," I said.

Jonas loved his nephew—his son. You had to spend only a few minutes with them to see that. It was the only reason I could think of that could explain why he had killed Leitha, because I was suddenly sure he had.

"Lachlan adored his mother and father and they felt the same way about him. If there were any fairness in the world, any justice, they would be alive and Leitha would have died years ago." He took a deep breath and slowly let it out. "It's her fault they're dead, you know," he said.

The lines around his mouth tightened. It was the only sign of what he was feeling. I suspected Jonas had learned to keep his emotions to himself a long time ago.

"Leitha kept pushing Colin to get more involved in the family business," he continued. "She still had shares in Black Dog and she convinced him to go and vote her proxy. The accident happened on the way home. She would have ruined every memory Lachlan had of them. I couldn't let her do that. And I couldn't let her cut him off from the trust money for his education."

My phone was on the table. There was no way I could reach it before he shot me. The only thing I could do was keep him talking. I was Miss Marple in the drawing room of an English country manor, I told myself. I was Hercule Poirot on the *Orient Express.*

"You laced your tea with potassium chloride and put sugar in it so Leitha wouldn't notice the taste."

"Potassium chloride tastes a little salty and slightly metallic, but the sugar hid that quite well," Jonas said. The shoulders of his jacket were damp. It must still be raining, I realized.

I put one hand on the back of the chair next to me, gripping it tightly so Jonas wouldn't see my hand shaking. "How did she figure it out?" I asked. I genuinely wanted to know the answer.

Jonas rubbed his face with his free hand. "It was that study she was part of. They were looking into the genetics of heart disease, looking to see if there was a connection to common physical traits like eye and hair color, and how cilantro tastes to someone. Leitha outlived her brother and lived longer than her parents and her grandparents. She had the Finnamore green eyes. They had become less common over the years."

I nodded. "I remember Mike saying that."

"She didn't want the Finnamore line to die out. It drove her crazy that Eloise had adopted instead of having biological children. I can't remember when she wasn't at Mike to get married and have babies. He'd just laugh and say one of him was enough for the world."

I almost smiled. I could imagine Mike saying that.

"And she was always pestering Colin and Ainsley to have more children. She didn't know that they had been trying for years to have a brother or sister for Lachlan. It just never happened."

I could see the pain in his eyes. "It was only one time with

Ainsley, a momentary lapse on both our parts. Colin was the only man for her."

"And she was the only one for you," I said. It was a guess but a good one.

He nodded.

Jonas had slept with his brother's wife—a huge betrayal. The fact that he had been in love with her forever probably would have made things worse if the truth had come out. But Lachlan was the result. How could Leitha even have considered telling him? It seemed too cruel even for her. As Jonas's child, Lachlan wasn't entitled to any money from the family trust because he was not a biological Finnamore. Did money really matter more to her?

"Did you know Lachlan was your child from the beginning?" I asked.

"Not at first. But when they couldn't seem to have more children, I got suspicious. I finally confronted Ainsley and she admitted that I was Lachlan's father. She didn't want him or Colin to know and neither did I. I didn't want to break up that family. Colin was Lachlan's father. The only father he knew. The only father that mattered. I didn't want to do that to my . . . to Lachlan and I never wanted Colin to know that I had betrayed him. I wanted to be the big brother he believed in."

"Leitha wasn't going to let Lachlan have the money for college from the trust."

Jonas shook his head. "The DNA shouldn't have mattered. Lachlan was Colin's child in all the ways that were important, but Leitha was the trustee and her belief was that only blood Finnamores were entitled to the money. Eloise's daughters should have gotten the money for their education as well. If Leitha wouldn't release the funds for her own grandchildren, she wasn't going to give it to Lachlan and she was determined to tell him why."

"So you decided to kill her," I said. How was I going to get out of this? What would Jonas do when he got to the end of his explanation?

"Yes," he said. "I won't insult you by saying I had no other choice. There were other options. I just didn't like any of them. I knew potassium chloride could bring on a heart attack. I started college as a chemistry major."

"Leitha gave you an ultimatum, didn't she?" I took a step closer to the chair and dropped my hand onto Owen's back. He meowed softly.

"She had given me forty-eight hours to tell Lachlan the truth or she said she would. On the day of Mary's presentation at the library, I had just a few hours left. She was a miserable old woman and the world isn't any worse off with her dead. It was easy to get the potassium chloride at the university. I faked drinking the tea when I was talking to Rebecca. It was that simple."

"And then Marcus got suspicious about two deaths so close together in one family."

"I really wish he hadn't done that," Jonas said. He looked like he felt bad, but the gun he was pointing at me didn't waver.

"When we were at Eric's, I knew the minute the words were out of my mouth that I'd made a mistake with that comment about not liking sweet things. I knew you'd pick up on that. Marcus had told me about the contents of Leitha's stomach. I knew he would have told you as well. And you don't miss details like that."

"So what happens now?" I said. I was surprised how steady my voice sounded since both of my hands were shaking and my chest felt as though an elephant had just sat on it.

"We're going for a ride," he said.

"Where?"

"Out to Wisteria Hill."

My heart sank. He'd heard my conversation with Roma when we'd been at Eric's.

He nodded his head as though he'd read my mind. "Yes, I heard enough of your conversation to know that Dr. Davidson and her husband won't be there. And I know that you're looking after the cats that live out there. For some reason you wanted to check on them tonight. It's been raining hard and you were just worried about them. You're a very kind person." His eyes hardened. He gestured with the gun. "Let's go."

"I need my keys."

"And bring your phone," Jonas said.

"All right," I said. I felt a frisson of hope. If I had my phone, there was a chance I could get help. I leaned down and kissed Owen on the top of my head. "It'll be okay," I whispered. I wasn't sure if the words were for his benefit or mine. At the

SOFIE KELLY

edge of my vision, I could see Hercules peeking around the living room doorway. At least they were both safe.

We walked out to the truck. "You drive please," Jonas said. He had such nice manners. How could someone who remembered to say "please" and "thank you" kill another person?

"I could put the car in the ditch," I said through clenched teeth as I fastened my seat belt. Anger was beginning to replace my fear.

"And I could shoot you," he said. "I think that puts us on even ground."

"If you're not going to shoot me, what are you going to do?" At least out at Wisteria Hill I had a chance. I knew the woods around Roma and Eddie's house well. Out there Jonas and I were no longer "on even ground." Out there I had an advantage.

"I told you, you're going to drive out to Wisteria Hill to check on the cats. You'll discover one of them is missing and you'll go looking for it in the dark and have a nasty and deadly fall into the brook."

"No, I won't," I said, forgetting for a moment that he was holding a gun on me.

His dark eyes narrowed. "If it comes down to choosing between Lachlan and you, between Lachlan and anyone, it's an easy decision."

I needed him to think about what he was doing. I needed him to think about what he had already done. That meant asking him the question I didn't want to hear the answer to. I tried to take a deep breath but I couldn't. My chest was tight with anger. Still I managed to get the words out. "Why did you kill Mike?"

He didn't say anything.

I glanced in his direction. The pain was raw on his face. Part of me felt compassion for the man and part of me wanted to hit him. I started the truck.

"I kind of understand about Leitha. I'm not saying what you did was right, but she threatened your child, so that part I get. But Mike would never have hurt Lachlan. Never."

"He didn't see that what he wanted to do would hurt Lachlan." His voice was flat, empty of emotion.

"Maybe Lachlan would be happy to find out he still had one parent," I said as I pulled out of the driveway.

"No. Lachlan adored Colin. He would be devastated to find out Colin wasn't his father." For a moment Jonas didn't speak but I could feel his gaze on me. "Mike was one of those people who saw the best in everyone and he had this idea that the rest of the world did the same thing. You're like that, too."

"He just wanted to tell the truth."

I saw Jonas nod his head out of the corner of my eye. "It was an accident," he said. "It wasn't like Leitha. Mike and I were arguing. He shoved me a couple of times and then I hit him back. He lost his balance and went backward. When I close my eyes, I can still see his head hit the mantel above the fireplace."

"I don't understand," I said. "Why didn't you call nine-one-one? It was an accident."

"He was dead."

I was gripping the steering wheel so tightly, I felt it might snap in half. "You're not a nurse or a doctor. You don't know that." Anger gave my voice a raspy harshness.

"I know how to check someone's pulse. He was dead. And I panicked. I wish I hadn't."

I glanced over at him again. The hand that was pointing the gun at me was shaking.

"I wish I hadn't punched him. I wish I hadn't gone over there. I wish I hadn't . . ." He didn't finish the sentence and I wondered if he'd been about to say he wished he hadn't slept with his sister-in-law.

We drove in silence for a few minutes. I needed to get Jonas talking again. I needed him to see me as a person and not an obstacle to be dealt with.

"Did Mike think Leitha might not have been a Finnamore?" I asked.

Jonas nodded. "You saw his notes. Yes. For a while he did. He found something in a diary of a midwife. Leitha was a surprise baby, coming years after her brother. She was supposed to have been born premature, but she was a robust eight pounds plus at birth according to the midwife."

"Her mother had an affair."

"Maybe. Celeste married John Finnamore on the rebound after a broken engagement. It seems she carried a torch for her former fiancé for the rest of her life."

"Mike tried to work out whether or not Leitha was a Finnamore by looking at eye color." We were almost at Wisteria Hill. All I could think was *Keep him talking.*

"The Finnamore green eyes," Jonas said. "It's ironic that Lachlan probably got his green eyes from me and I'm not a real Finnamore."

He was still holding on to my phone. He looked at it and then set it on the floor by his feet. "Eye color was just too complicated. Too many factors involved. Then Mike looked at the type of everyone's hair, which told him that Leitha *was* a Finnamore—her mother's previous beau had straight hair."

"Which meant Leitha would have had wavy hair, not curly," I said.

He nodded. "But the old eye-color thing had him intrigued. He was trying to work out when green eyes first showed up in the family tree. He wouldn't let it go. He wanted us all to take those DNA tests so we'd know more about our genetic makeup. I couldn't dissuade him."

"You were afraid the truth would come out if Lachlan did the test."

"I gave him every logical reason not to that I could. You know what Mike was like. He told me I was too much of a worrier and everything would be fine."

"He got suspicious because you were so adamant."

"No," Jonas said.

I saw him shake his head out of the corner of my eye. I didn't believe him. I'd seen what Mike was like when he sank his teeth into something, the way he had been with researching his family tree. He wouldn't let go until every question he had was answered.

"He went back to his Punnett squares," I said, "while he was trying to change your mind. And at some point he started looking at everyone's hair again."

"People have always commented on Lachlan's curly hair. It's been like that since he was a baby."

"But his hair isn't curly. It's actually wavy. Curly hair is spiral and wavy is S-shaped. The interesting thing is that hair type is an example of what's called incomplete dominance. It means that if you have one of each version of the gene, you end up with a mix of the two: not straight, not curly, but wavy hair."

"I see why Mike liked you," Jonas said.

"What do you mean?"

"You're a lot alike. You notice things other people don't. And you have a strong sense of right and wrong."

He was right. Were our similarities going to get me killed, too?

"I couldn't let the truth come out. I wanted Lachlan to at least be able to get an education."

"Why didn't you just pay for college yourself?" I looked over at him again.

"I can't. Without the trust there is no money for Lachlan's education. There isn't even enough money to hang on to the house much longer."

"I don't understand."

"It took every cent Colin and Ainsley had to pay for her care after the accident. It took every cent I had and everything I could beg or borrow. Lachlan is as entitled to that trust money as anyone."

"So you finally just told Mike the truth." My eyes were on the road but I could watch him in my peripheral vision. The gun was still pointed at me.

"The night he . . . That night . . . Yes. He didn't think it was such a big deal. He told me we'd figure out college. Lachlan could take out a loan or better yet we could challenge the terms of the trust. He didn't understand that it would blow up Lachlan's life. I swear to God, I didn't mean for him to get hurt."

We were almost at Wisteria Hill. There wasn't anything left to talk about. I felt something brush against my leg then, as light as the sweep of a feather. I froze, my entire body rigid.

Owen. It had to be.

Owen was with us in the truck.

Jonas suddenly leaned forward. I forced myself to keep my eyes on the road. There was no way he could know that Owen was here. Even if the cat accidentally touched him. I could feel my pulse pounding in the hollow at the base of my throat and I made myself take deep breaths and slow down my breathing. Panicking wasn't going to do me any good.

"Detective Gordon sent you a text," Jonas said.

Marcus rarely sent texts. Had he figured out something was wrong? "What does it say?"

"He wants to know where you are."

I swallowed to ease my suddenly dry mouth. "Are you going to answer him?" I asked.

"No," he said.

We drove in silence for maybe a minute; then Jonas spoke again. "I'm sorry I have to do this."

"Then don't do it."

"And what? You'll give me your word that you'll keep all my secrets? You won't. As I said, you're just like Mike." There was an edge of anger to his voice now.

"No, I won't keep your secrets, but I will help you in any other way that I can."

He laughed. "You're honest. I'll give you that. But I would sacrifice my life for Lachlan. And yours as well. Detective Gordon is a good man. I'm sorry he's going to be hurt."

Not if I can help it, I said silently.

chapter 20

We were at Wisteria Hill. I drove slowly up the driveway, hoping that somehow Roma had been late leaving or that her plans had changed, but the farmhouse was in darkness. I parked as close to the old carriage house as I could.

"Give me the keys, please," Jonas said.

I handed them to him and laid one hand on the dashboard for a moment. Harrison had given me the truck because Owen and I had found some papers about his daughter, Elizabeth's, adoption. And we'd almost gotten blown up in the process. We had barely gotten clear of the cabin where we'd been trapped when the propane tank exploded. I remembered having no sense of where my body was as the impact propelled me into the brush. I had landed flat on my back in a pile of snow, cold, wet, bruised and bloody.

But alive.

And then I'd caught sight of Owen coming toward me, snow and bits of tree bark stuck to his fur, spitting angry, meowing loudly all the way.

But alive.

We'd gotten out of that and we were going to get out of this as well.

Jonas gestured with the gun and I climbed out of the truck. Could I sprint to the carriage house if I had the chance? I hoped so. From there the woods were dense enough that I could find lots of places to hide.

I stood next to the truck while Jonas stuffed the keys and my phone into his pocket. He'd said that I noticed things that other people didn't. He was right, which meant I'd paid attention when Harry had explained how he'd hot-wired a truck almost identical to this one when he was a lovestruck teenager. I didn't need those keys to get out of here.

"If I had any other option to protect Lachlan, I would take it," Jonas said. "Everything I have ever done has been for Lachlan."

"So tell the truth for Lachlan. Tell him who he really is."

"He's Colin and Ainsley's son. He's a Finnamore."

I wasn't going to get though to him. In a different circumstance, I would have respected his loyalty to his child. But I was in this circumstance.

"I admire you and people who are like you," he said. "I admire the fact that you truly do seem to see and expect the best from people, but I'm not like that. Maybe I was once, but not now. As I said before, I am sorry." Once more he gestured with the gun.

I thought about Marcus and Mom and Dad and Ethan and Sarah and Harrison and Roma and Maggie and the furballs. I thought about what Mary had taught me about kickboxing and the structure of the human knee.

"I'm sorry, too," I said.

And then I kicked the side of his knee as hard as I could. He yelled and went down, the hand holding the gun flying up in the air. I didn't waste any time trying to look for the gun. I ran and hoped Owen was with me.

I bolted around the side of the old carriage house and sprinted for the trees. I had a bit of a head start, but I knew it wasn't enough to let me double back to the truck. Jonas was taller and faster and stronger. I just hoped I'd connected hard enough that his knee would cause him enough trouble to give me an edge.

I tried to picture the road that ran in front of Wisteria Hill. If I turned left once I got up the graded embankment behind the carriage house, I could make another left turn and then head down toward the road. It made more sense than continuing to cut through the woods in the direction of the back access road. The main road would have more traffic.

It was dark and the air was heavy with moisture but it had

stopped raining. Everything was dripping. The ground was saturated with water. I was breathing heavily. My feet in my canvas shoes were already soaking wet. I could hear the sound of rushing water. There was a stream off to the left behind the carriage house, skirting the rise where the trees began. When I got that far, I would need to turn left a second time. I reminded myself that it didn't matter that it was dark. I could hear the water. I knew which way to go. I had an advantage Jonas didn't have.

Owen still hadn't appeared. I was afraid to even whisper the cat's name in case Jonas heard me. I had to keep moving forward, hoping that Owen was here somewhere in the darkness beside me.

I made my way through the dripping trees, trying not to lose my footing on the mud and leaves and pine needles underfoot. Climbing up the embankment was a challenge. My feet kept sliding out from under me. The water sounded louder, closer. I tried to picture the last time I'd been here earlier in the summer. I couldn't be that far from the stream. I could follow it to the road. I just had to keep moving.

I went from one tree to the next, hugging their trunks, trying to stay small and quiet. I had to assume Jonas was behind me. And then suddenly I pitched forward. A tree branch snapped against my forehead and I landed facedown on the ground. I rolled over onto my back, trying to get my breath. After a few moments, I sat up, running one hand down my right leg. The calf, right above my ankle, was bleeding. I flexed my foot and grimaced. It hurt but I didn't think anything was broken. I felt around on the ground. I had tripped over a sharp-edged rock a bit bigger than my hand.

I could feel blood running down my leg. I needed a bandage. I pulled off my shirt, grateful that I had a tank top underneath. I managed to tear the fabric at a side seam. I tore off the whole right-front section and fashioned a makeshift tourniquet, knotting it as tightly as I could around my leg. I had just tied a second knot when Owen appeared beside me. He nuzzled my hand and I had to swallow a couple of times so I wouldn't cry. I buried my face in his neck. He was muddy and wet and none too happy.

The rock I'd tripped over was still next to my foot. I ran my fingers over it and thought maybe I could use it. I looked around. Even though it was dark, I could see that I was at the upper edge of the embankment. I listened, focusing on tuning out the water rushing over the rocks. I heard a foot slip on the wet ground. Or was it just a racoon or a skunk? No. They would have been more sure-footed. It had to be Jonas. He was quiet but not quiet enough.

I kissed the top of Owen's head, hoping he'd understand what I wanted him to do. I pointed at a nearby tree and then held up the rock. I pantomimed throwing it. He cocked his head to one side. Then I pointed to him and mimicked throwing back my head and yowling. My face was close to his and I saw his golden eyes narrow. Did he get it? I needed him to draw Jonas over to us. He probably would come this way but I needed to be sure and I needed to be ready.

My heart was pounding. My plan to get away from a man who wanted to kill me depended on a cat playing his part. But Owen wasn't just any cat. I climbed the tree, grateful that it was wet and made my progress quieter. I slid out along a branch about eight feet up, holding the rock tightly with one hand. I pushed my damp hair out of my face and gestured in Owen's direction. His response was to take a couple of swipes at his face with his paw. For a moment I thought he hadn't understood me and then he meowed loudly. He leaned forward and he meowed again and then again.

I was counting on the fact that even though he had killed two people, there was still some part of Jonas Quinn that was a good, kind person. My heart was thumping so hard, I was afraid it would shake me off the branch. The gash on my leg throbbed and the edge of the rock dug into my hand. Then Jonas came through the trees. I didn't see any sign of the gun. Either he hadn't found it after I'd kicked him, or he hadn't bothered looking. Owen meowed once more and to my surprise held up one paw. Was he . . . acting?

Jonas looked around; then he sighed. "What are you doing way out here? You belong down with the other cats."

He thought Owen was part of the feral colony. Owen continued to hold up his paw, his meows becoming more pitiful.

Jonas took a step closer. "I'll come back for you," he said.

It was now or never. I calculated the angle, hoped my math was right and then pushed myself partway up with my free arm and threw the rock with everything I had.

The rock struck Jonas on the side of his head, just above his right temple. His legs buckled and he collapsed. I waited for a moment to see if he'd move. When he didn't, I made my way down out of the tree, slipping on the wet bark and almost landing on the ground next to Jonas. I had scraped the skin on one arm but I was all right. I could see his chest moving ,so I knew Jonas was breathing.

I grabbed Owen. "We're okay," I said. "We're okay." My makeshift bandage was soaked through with blood and my leg hurt but I knew I could retrace my steps back to the truck. I'd crawl if I had to.

I took two steps and Jonas's arm snaked out and grabbed my ankle, pulling me down. I fell hard, knocking the wind out of me. Owen had jumped from my arms and stood by my head hissing as I struggled to catch my breath.

I kicked, gasping for air, and tried to roll over and sit up but Jonas was already on his feet. He grabbed my other leg and began dragging me across the ground. I yelled for help. I tried to grab onto anything, a tree root, a rock, a bush, but he was bigger and stronger.

He was headed for the stream. He was going to push me over the edge onto the rocks and into the water. Panic swirled in my chest. I used the burst of adrenaline to twist and kick even harder. It didn't work. Jonas's hands were clamped around my ankles like a set of handcuffs. I couldn't see Owen anymore, but I could hear him. I wasn't sure if he'd disappeared or was just out of my line of sight.

My face banged against the ground and I got a mouthful of dirt. I spit and choked. I couldn't get away. I could try to pull Jonas over with me or I could do everything I could to survive the fall. I stopped kicking and flailing. I went limp, hoping Jonas might loosen his grip even a little. I couldn't seem to stop shaking, but I promised myself that when he pushed me, I'd curl into a ball and cover my head with my arms. I'd probably break some bones, but as long as I stayed conscious, I'd be all right. I was a good swimmer and the water was high, but it wouldn't be cold. I would get out of this.

We were at the edge of the gully. Jonas let go of one of my ankles. I tried to kick him but he dodged my foot.

"Get up," he said.

I still had dirt in my mouth, my arms were scraped and I could feel blood running down my leg. I knew physically I was no match for Jonas but I wasn't getting to my feet. I wasn't helping him throw me over.

"No," I said.

He bent down and grabbed my arm, pulling me halfway off the ground. Pain sliced through my left side but I forced myself to go limp again, and as my body slumped forward, I bit his hand.

He let go and I scrambled backward. Owen appeared claws out and hissing. When Jonas came toward me, I used my good leg to kick him in the stomach. I fell to my knees. Jonas doubled over for a moment and I thought he was going to go down again. He swayed but stayed on his feet and pulled the gun out of his pocket. So he had found it. I was out of options.

Jonas pointed the gun at me. I lifted my chin and stared up at him and behind me Marcus shouted, "Drop the gun!"

For a long moment Jonas didn't move.

"Drop the gun," Marcus called out again. "It's over. Just put it down."

Finally, Jonas nodded. He lowered his arm and leaned forward, setting the gun on the ground. I got to my feet, never taking my eyes off of his face. I felt Marcus's strong arms go around me, pulling me against his chest.

"Are you all right?" he said.

I nodded because I didn't trust my voice to work. Jonas took a step backward.

"Stay where you are," Marcus said.

Jonas took another step backward.

"It's over."

Jonas nodded. "I know." He looked at me. "Kathleen, tell Lachlan he was the great joy of my life. Tell him that Ainsley and Colin loved him."

I realized what he was going to do but it was too late.

He jumped.

The next few hours were a blur. Marcus called for backup and wrapped his jacket around my shoulders. He climbed down to the water but Jonas was dead.

We drove to the hospital and Marcus flashed his badge to get me seen right away. The gash on my leg and a cut on my forehead needed stitches. Dirt had to be cleaned out of all my scraped skin. The doctor said my ribs weren't broken. Bruises were already darkening on my left side. But I *was* alive.

Marcus left Owen in the car with the window cracked and a chicken salad sandwich he'd gotten from the vending machine in the waiting room.

"How did you know where I was?" I asked while we waited for the nurse to come back with a prescription and instructions on how to take care of the cut on my leg.

It turned out that Owen had managed to respond to Marcus's text with a string of nonsense letters and symbols. "I knew you had to be in trouble," he said.

"What made you come out to Wisteria Hill?"

"Hercules. He was pacing back and forth in the kitchen. You know that photo you have on the refrigerator of Roma and Eddie the day they got married?"

I nodded. "He knocked it to the ground. Then he picked it up and brought it to me. I was looking for any clue in the house and he brought me the picture three times. Quinn's car was parked up the street. I ran the plates. It was just too much of a coincidence and then I realized what Hercules was trying to tell me."

I stretched out my arm and caught his hand.

"He killed Leitha," Marcus said. "He was the only person I couldn't eliminate. I figured it had to have been the tea."

"It was," I said. "He just pretended to drink it. Lachlan was his child, not his brother, Colin's. Leitha figured it out."

Marcus shook his head.

I swallowed a couple of times. "He killed Mike, too."

He stared at me. His mouth worked but no words came out at first. "No," he finally managed to say.

"I'm sorry," I said. I told him everything Jonas had told me. "I don't think it was just about the Finnamore money. I think he genuinely thought he would lose Lachlan if the truth came out."

Marcus pulled one hand down over the back of his neck. "This is worse."

"I know," I said softly.

chapter 21

One of the nurses found a set of scrubs for me. They were a bit big, but they were clean and I didn't have to leave in one of those gowns that flapped open in the back. Owen was stretched out on the middle of the backseat of Marcus's SUV, asleep with one paw over his nose.

"I can't believe he texted you," I said.

Marcus shrugged. "He can disappear whenever he feels like it. Texting doesn't seem like that big of a stretch."

"Why did you text me in the first place? You always call."

"I did call," he said as he unlocked the passenger door and helped me get settled on the seat. "It went to voice mail. I'm guessing Quinn turned off the ringer as well."

Owen lifted his head, murped hello and came from the backseat to the front, settling himself on my lap. He nuzzled my chin and I stroked his fur.

"You were very brave," I told him, "and very smart."

Marcus leaned down and kissed the top of my head. "So were you," he said.

When we pulled into the driveway, Hercules came around the side of the house as though he'd been listening for the sound of the SUV. I opened the car door and Owen jumped from my lap to the ground. Marcus came and helped me to my feet. I leaned down over his protests and picked up Hercules. He studied my face, green eyes narrowed.

"I'm fine," I said, kissing his furry head. "You saved us. Thank you for telling Marcus where we were."

"Mrr," he said, his nose touching mine.

"I love you, too," I whispered.

We made our way around the house to the back door with Owen leading the way. Marcus unlocked the door and I had the feeling he would have carried me into the kitchen if I'd let him.

"I'm all right," I said, reaching up to put my hand to his cheek. "I knew you'd find me."

He pressed his lips together before he spoke. "I thought he was going to throw you over the side of the gully," he said, a rough edge to his voice.

"He was. But I had a plan."

He looked at me for a long moment. Then he started to

laugh, wrapping both arms tightly around me. "I love you," he said.

I felt my throat get tight at the thought that I might never have heard those words again. "I love you, too," I whispered.

Marcus had to head back to Wisteria Hill and he had no intention of leaving me alone even though I protested that I had Owen and Hercules. Turned out, he'd already called Rebecca. She arrived at the door with one of her poultices for the tub, some poached salmon for the boys and a basket of still warm blueberry muffins.

Marcus kissed me twice, told Rebecca to call if I needed anything and instructed Owen and Hercules to watch me. Then he left.

"Oh, sweet girl, I am so glad you're all right," Rebecca said, and I saw the gleam of unshed tears in her eyes. She took my hands in hers and turned them over to examine the scraped-raw skin. I saw her wince. She eyed my forehead. "Does that hurt?" she asked.

I shook my head. "Not very much. They gave me some pills at the hospital."

She reached up and brushed my hair back off of my face. Something about that simple gesture made me start to tremble.

"Jonas killed Leitha," I said in a voice that trembled, too. "He killed Mike. Mike."

"But he didn't kill you," she said.

I started to cry and she folded me into her arms and I cried for everyone who was lost and everyone who was still here.

I woke up looking worse than I felt. I discovered Marcus in the kitchen making coffee with two furry helpers with suspiciously fishy breath. All three of them were insistent that I needed to stay home.

I didn't put up much of an argument. Marcus went out to feed the cats at my insistence. Maggie arrived with a cream for my bruises—Rebecca had been teaching Maggie the things Rebecca herself had learned from her own mother for quite some time now. Owen was overjoyed to see her. She praised both cats for their resourcefulness and bravery.

"I think you're part cat yourself," she said, hugging me as though she thought I might break. "You've used up at least three or four of your nine lives."

I couldn't stop thinking about Lachlan. Marcus had told me that he was with Johnny and Ritchie and Elena Gonzalez. The band had closed ranks around him. Eloise had defied her doctor's orders about flying and would be arriving in the late afternoon. After supper Marcus and I were going to share the details of the story that weren't public knowledge with them all, including the truth about Lachlan's parentage. I was trying not to think about how painful that conversation was going to be, but secrets were why all of this had happened. Secrets were why Mike and Leitha—and Jonas—were dead.

I was sitting in the backyard in the sunshine just before lunch, with my leg propped up on an overturned laundry basket, while Maggie and Owen picked tomatoes, when Harrison and Harry came around the side of the house.

I started to get up but the old man raised a hand. "Don't even think about moving," he said.

I smiled up at him. "What are you doing here?" I asked.

"I wanted to see for myself that you're all right."

"I'm fine, I promise."

For a long moment Harrison didn't say anything. He took in the bandage on my leg, the stitches on my forehead and the various scrapes and bruises that were visible. Then he shook his head. "I'm so damn sorry for getting you involved in all of this," he said.

I was shaking my head before he had all the words out. "No, no, no. Nothing that happened is your fault. Mike was my friend, too." I put one hand on my chest. I thought about Jonas dragging me toward the edge of the gully. Those could have been the last moments of my life. They had been the last moments of Jonas's life. I took a breath. "What I did was my choice. What Jonas did was his."

One month and three days later, I was backstage at the Stratton Theatre, which was sold out for the Stars and Garters burlesque revival.

"They sound like a rowdy bunch," Maggie said as we peeked out at the crowd. She grinned. "This is going to be fun."

True to her promise to Roma, she was taking part in the show. She wore fishnets, high heels and a very short, barely there frilly white dress, and she was carrying a shepherd's hook.

"Every guy out there is going to lose their mind over you," I said. "The Little Bo-Peep in my book of Mother Goose stories did not look like this."

Mary was acting as mistress of ceremonies. She passed us all in black satin, carrying a huge feathered headdress like they'd wear in a show in Vegas. "It's not too late to be onstage, Kathleen," she said over her shoulder.

"I already did my part," I called after her.

Roma peeked out at the crowd, then grabbed my arm. "Are you sure this is a good idea?" she asked. We were about fifteen minutes from the curtain going up.

I laughed. "As my mother likes to say, 'If you have to dance with a bear, put on your high heels and tango.'"

"I take it that means yes?" Roma said.

I hugged her. "Times three!"

There were hoots and good-natured catcalls and waves of applause for each act. It was clear the show was a hit. I headed down to the dressing room to check on what Mary called our showstopper.

I'd taken two steps into the room when Brady grabbed my arm. "My shirt is missing half the buttons," he said.

"Your shirt is fine," I said. "Just put it on."

I clapped my hands. "You have five minutes, everyone."

"Kathleen, I can't go out in public in this outfit," Harry said in a low voice. His shirt was just like the one Brady had been complaining about and like Brady he didn't have it on.

"Of course you can." I pulled at the sleeve of his white T-shirt. "And you need to take this shirt off."

He pointed at himself with one finger. "Nobody wants to see this without a shirt on."

"People paid good money to see that. All of that," I said. "Don't make me take that T-shirt off of you, Harry Taylor." I gave him my best stern-librarian look. "Mary taught me a few moves. I can do it."

He took a step backward.

I held up four fingers. "Four minutes," I said.

A hand touched my shoulder. I turned around to see Marcus standing there. At least he had his shirt on.

"You so owe me for this," he said.

Silver lamé and sequins had never looked so good. "I can live with that." I told him. And then I winked.

To me, Zorro belonged to Mike and Mike alone. The show needed something that would celebrate the spirit of the man, but not be a pale imitation of his act. And then I remembered what Mike had called out to the crowd at the concert—*C'mon, people, you should be dancin'!*—and I knew what to do.

Ella King had made the guys' outfits with help from Rebecca, and the two of them had used every sequin within a five-mile radius of Mayville Heights. Rebecca had jokingly asked Ella if she could make an extra outfit for Everett—at least I was telling myself she was joking.

Finally Mary walked onstage to introduce the last act. "At our first show our star act was the dashing Zorro and we all miss him very much." She unveiled a large photo of Mike dancing in his costume. "Mike Bishop's absence has left a huge hole in this show and in our lives. Anyone who spent even five minutes with the man knew how much he loved music. So we honor his memory and celebrate his life with Mike's own words: 'You should be dancin'!'"

The throbbing disco percussion of the Bee Gees' hit began to pound in the background.

The guys came out in their silver disco outfits: tight flared pants, boots with heels, chunky silver neck chains and sequinned shirts open to the navel because there weren't any buttons above that. Sandra Godfrey had spent two hours with them working on a routine. She'd walked into the library afterward, laid her head on the circulation desk and said, "They're all hopeless. They have no rhythm, no sense of timing. You know that saying 'You've gotta dance like nobody's watching'? Well, the whole town will be watching and they can't dance!"

She was right, but it didn't matter. All five of them were stiff and awkward at first, but Johnny was the consummate performer. He started to swivel his hips Elvis style, and before I knew it, he was doing a hip bump with Eddie.

Marcus, Brady and Harry were doing their version of disco;

at least I thought that was what it was. One hand was on their hips as their other arm pointed sideways à la John Travolta in *Saturday Night Fever*. That was followed by an arm roll and a repeat on the other side. They were even more or less in sync.

I realized that Brady was repeating something over and over. Maybe Sandra had taught them more than she'd thought. I watched his lips. Maybe she hadn't. Brady was a football fan like his dad. He was saying, "False start, defense, false start, offense." The movements all lined up. And it didn't matter that they were more NFL referees than disco stars because the audience loved them.

Sandra moaned and leaned against me. "Someone is going to put this on the Internet and John Travolta is going to sue me," she said.

I would have answered her but I was laughing too hard. And if a couple of tears got mixed in, that was okay, too. Mike would have loved this, I was certain. Once again, I was watching a show where the crowd went wild and I fervently hoped that wherever or whatever Mike Bishop was in the universe, he, too, was dancing.

acknowledgments

It takes a multitude of people working diligently behind the scenes at the publisher to make my books the best they can be and then help readers find them. Thank you, everyone. Special thanks to my talented editor, Jessica Wade, who always finds all the holes I've left in the story. Her skills make every book better. Thank you as well to assistant editor, Miranda Hill, who keeps us all on track.

My agent, Kim Lionetti, is everything a writer could want—advocate, cheerleader and wisewoman. Thanks, Kim!

A big thank-you goes to the real Dr. Michael Bishop, endodontist extraordinaire, and his staff who have always taken excellent care of this very anxious patient. Dr. B. never played the stand-up bass in a church band, wore his hair in a mullet or danced in a burlesque show—at least as far as I know. He is, however, a very good sport.

And last but never least, thank you to Patrick and Lauren who always have my back and my heart.